Praise for *ONCE A DETECTIVE...*

"Larry Terhaar's Once a Detective is a masterfully plotted mystery with a compelling narrative voice, vividly drawn characters, and sizzling dialogue. A nuanced, emotion-filled portrayal of a struggling ex-cop who becomes a private eye, this novel is much more than a simple whodunit. It is impossible not to become immersed in the story—the book will grip you from beginning to end."

— Urs A. Boelsterli, award-winning author of *"Dead Natural"*

"Once a Detective," is a fast-paced romp through the streets of New York by former Detective Dan Burnett, in search of a killer. Larry Terhaar is a great storyteller. His characters were well developed and compelling. I could feel the grit from the streets and taste the flavors of the fabulous food described. A fun summer read with lots of action."

— John W. Long, author of *"In the Name of the Father."*

"Larry Terhaar excels in weaving mystery with personal growth and revelations. This approach gives his story the added flavor and value of unexpected insights and conclusions that many readers won't see coming. The heady mix of interpersonal and professional growth permeates the story, building an atmosphere that relies on more than intrigue alone to cement its attraction."

— D. Donovan, Sr. Reviewer, Midwest Book Review

AGAINST THE BLUE WALL

A Dan Burnett Thriller

BY

LARRY TERHAAR

Copyright © 2025 by Larry Terhaar

All rights reserved.

Formatting provided by Trisha Fuentes

This is a work of fiction. Unless otherwise indicated, all the names, characters, businesses, places, events, and incidents in this book are either the product of the author's imagination or used in a fictitious manner. Any resemblance to actual persons, living or dead is purely coincidental.

ISBN: 979-8-9900362-2-2 (Paperback)

DEDICATION

In the history of the United States, for every Rodney King, George Floyd, or Tyre Nichols, thousands more Black men have been beaten or killed by the police.

It is those people to whom this book is dedicated.

CONTENT WARNING:

This book contains depictions of racial violence that may be distressing for some readers. Themes of Discrimination, brutality, and systemic racism are explored in multiple passages within the narrative. Reader discretion is advised.

This is a work of fiction. While it takes place in real locations, primarily in Westchester County, New York, the author has no knowledge or suspicions of any crimes described in this story occurring there. Incidents and characters' names are the product of the author's imagination and are used fictitiously. Any resemblance to actual events or persons, living or dead, is entirely coincidental.

CHAPTER 1

Officer Sean O'Riley

"License and registration, please."

As the driver opened the glove compartment, O'Riley said, "Put both hands on the wheel, boy," drew his weapon, and asked Maddox if he saw a gun.

The driver did as he was told and said, "I don't have a gun."

Until then, Maddox had been watching for traffic and not looking into the vehicle. The question got his attention, though, and he looked into the car at the glove compartment.

"I don't see anything," Maddox said.

"I saw a gun," O'Riley insisted.

Five minutes earlier, an hour after sunset, their patrol car was parked on the west side of North Broadway, just south of the Route 287 exit ramps. The engine was running with the heat on as Officers Sean O'Riley, a twenty-year veteran of the White Plains Police Department, and John Maddox, with just one year of service, were in the middle of the four p.m. to midnight shift.

The spot they chose was a park-like entrance to some office buildings set back from the well-traveled road. When they were not responding to a call, they often sat here looking for traffic violations—speeding, driving under the influence, whatever. It had been a boring shift, and they had yet to write a ticket when a Honda Accord passed by heading south. As it passed under a street light, O'Riley could see a young Black man driving and began to follow. They had not witnessed any violations, and his speed was below the limit. A half-mile later, the Honda changed lanes to pass a slow-moving truck without using a signal.

"Let's light him up, John. Maybe we can smell alcohol or marijuana in the car," O'Riley said.

With the lights flashing but no siren, they moved closer behind the Honda as they approached the center of town. Before the next traffic light, the vehicle pulled over into the parking lane near Tibbets Park and stopped along the curb. O'Riley pulled in behind the Honda, exited the patrol car, and approached the open driver's side window, with Officer Maddox two steps behind.

"What did I do?" the young Black man asked.

O'Riley felt the first twinge of excitement in his belly, then asked, "Do you have any drugs in the car?"

"What?" was the reply.

"That was a yes or no question."

"No."

So far, the driver had yet to address O'Riley with a sir, officer, or other sign of respect, which he thought he deserved, and his excitement grew stronger.

Officer Maddox drew his service weapon with his right hand, opened the driver's door with his left, and ordered, "Out of the car, please."

O'Riley moved forward to make room for the opening door while keeping his weapon aimed at the driver's head. As the driver nervously exited the vehicle with his hands raised, Maddox closed the door and said, "Turn around and put your hands on the roof."

As the young Black man complied with the order, O'Riley's excitement consumed him, and tiny beads of sweat formed on his forehead. After Maddox returned his weapon to its holster, he removed the cuffs from his belt, pulled the driver's hands behind his back, snapped the cuffs on his wrists, and pushed him against the car.

With his weapon holstered, Officer O'Riley struck the driver on the right side of the head with his nightstick using full force. He then turned, took a two- handed grip on the club, and swung back the other way, striking him on the left side of the head.

The driver yelled, "Take it easy, man!" with his head hunched between his shoulders for protection as the beating continued.

Maddox exclaimed, "Sean, we're in the middle of town. There are people around!"

"I don't care. This is our chance to beat this animal when he can't fight back. Take some shots, man!" O'Riley said, now possessed and breathing rapidly, sweat dripping off his face.

Using his fists, Maddox swung at the driver's head and shoulders as the young man bent over to protect himself. After a few more blows from O'Riley's nightstick, the driver slumped lower and finally collapsed on the street. O'Riley began kicking him in the ribs while Maddox continued striking his head until the young Black man was unconscious.

Once the two cops had caught their breath, they dragged him toward the front of the car and propped him up against the tire while his head hung lifelessly against his chest. O'Riley kicked his ribs one last time while Maddox returned to the patrol car to call it in.

Officer Sean O'Riley stood over the young man, relishing the feeling of conquest. It had been a while since he had felt the elation he so desperately needed, the reason he had become a cop: to put down these Black savages at every opportunity.

CHAPTER 2

Dan Burnett

As I opened my eyes to the first signs of daylight peering through the drapes, my gaze led me to Mia's angelic face, sleeping beside me. We were in her big bed in a grand old house that overlooked Long Island Sound in Mamaroneck, New York. Being careful not to wake her, I reached for my phone on the nightstand, saw it was 7:30, and noticed a new email from Seth Bodner, an attorney I knew from a previous case. He had recently represented the woman who murdered Mia's brother a few years ago.

My name is Dan Burnett. Six months ago, I became a private detective after retiring from a thirty-year career with the NYPD. I'm still in pretty good shape for fifty-five, other than a bad back that acts up from time to time, which was the reason for my retirement. I slid my lanky six-foot-three, one-hundred- eighty-pound body out of bed and silently walked into the bathroom, which was opulent compared to the one on my sailboat, where, until lately, I spent most of my nights. Her bathroom was all marble with a huge soaking tub and a glassed- in shower that was big enough for two. At least.

After brushing my teeth, shaving, and combing my thick brown hair, I paused to take stock of my face and noticed the signs of aging. My eyes seemed deeper set, and the first signs of gray hair had appeared at my temples. I stared for another moment, resigned to the fact there was nothing I could do about it, and made my way downstairs to the kitchen.

While waiting for the coffee to brew, I looked out over the Sound and sensed the sun's intensity strengthening now, the first week of March 2024. This was the first hint that spring was coming, which reminded me of everything I needed to do to prepare my boat for the season.

While taking my first sips of coffee and gazing out at the water, I imagined taking Mia sailing with me and looking up at her house from the water. We met last fall when Privateer, my boat and my home, was all buttoned up at the dock for the winter.

It was just a usual day in October when Mia walked into the office that I shared with my partner, Jim Abbott. After telling me about her brother being murdered two years ago and how the NYPD had recently given up on the case, she hired me on the spot to find his killer. I was immediately attracted to her but fought the temptation to get involved while she was my client. Fighting that temptation became more challenging over time, and after solving the case, a passionate affair ensued. Since then, we have become a couple and declared our love for one another. Considering the winters in New York and my living conditions aboard the boat, it's been my good fortune to have this wonderful home to spend my nights.

I read Seth Bodner's email, which was just a request to call him regarding a new case, and thought it best to wait until nine. A moment later, Mia appeared next to me in a luxurious silky robe, rose up on her toes, and kissed me.

"Good morning, love," she said while hugging me.

"Good morning, sweetheart."

After releasing me, she poured herself a cup and stood alongside me, taking in the bright morning as the sunlight reflected the gold and green sparkles in her eyes. It took little imagination to be aware of Mia's perfect, youthful body under her robe. She's seven years younger than me and is one of those women who looks just as good in the morning as she does when all dressed up for an evening on the town. Even then, she wears minimal makeup and drapes her long brown hair over her shoulders.

I told her about Seth's email, and we both wondered what it could be about. A few minutes after 9:00, I called his office while Mia was getting dressed.

"Hello, Dan. Thanks for calling back."

"Sure, Seth. What can I do for you?"

"I'm representing Jerome Jordan's family. I'm sure you know who he is?"

"Of course," I replied. Jerome Jordan was a young Black man who was beaten severely by two cops during a traffic stop in White Plains a few days ago. Since then, the news has been dominated by the story, not just in New York but nationwide. There were protests and marches on the streets of White Plains and Manhattan. Civil rights leaders led the marches and appeared on TV around the clock.

Seth explained, "The police, so far, have refused to release any video from bodycams or the patrol car, so we have no verification of what led to his beating. He's still unconscious and unable to tell his side of the story."

"Is he going to make it?" I asked.

"The doctors are hopeful. They won't know until the brain swelling goes down."

"How can I help?"

"We need to find some video footage from other sources. I'm hoping you can hunt that down for us."

"I'm certainly willing to try. I assume you have the police report?"

"I do," Seth replied.

"How about I stop by your office today for a copy of whatever you have, and I'll bring one of my standard terms of engagement. Does 1:00 work for you?"

"Perfect, see you then, Dan."

Shortly after ending the call, Mia returned to the kitchen, dressed for the day.

"Jerome Jordan's family has retained Seth. He wants me to do some investigating for him," I said.

"Really?" Her face lit up. "How exciting to work on a high-profile case like that. Everyone in the country is following it!"

"It is, but I hope to keep a low profile."

"I understand, but it still sounds exciting."

"I'm meeting with Seth this afternoon."

"Good luck with it, love. I'm leaving shortly to go shopping and have lunch with my sister. Will you return in time for dinner?"

"I hope to. I'll let you know if I'm not."

"Okay. I'll pick up something for us then," Mia said as she leaned over to kiss me before heading out the door.

"Enjoy your lunch with Judy!" I called out as she left.

While driving my Jeep Grand Cherokee to Seth's office in White Plains, I realized how this event with Jerome Jordan had triggered my anger about racism in our country. My mind went back to the video of Rodney King in California years ago and the shame I felt while watching it. Over the years since, I realized the shame came from just being a white man in a country with a history of slavery. And the fact that I was a member of a police force made me feel even more guilty watching them use their authority to do what they did. Ever since seeing that, I've felt a duty to ensure that it never happened in my presence or anywhere I could put a stop to it.

I wallowed in those feelings until my phone rang, then smiled when an image of my daughter's face popped up on the screen.

"Hi, Hannah. How's it going?"

"Everything's fine, Dad. I haven't heard from you all week, so I thought I'd check in."

"I was just thinking about preparing Privateer for the season; it finally feels like spring."

"I know, that's what prompted my call. Let me know when you need some help."

"Thanks for offering. I'll need help putting the sails on in a few weeks.

How about dinner some night?"

"Sure—maybe tomorrow?"

"Sounds good. I'll call in the morning to confirm," I replied. "Okay. Talk to you then. Love you!"

"Bye, Han. Love you, too!"

Hannah is twenty-one and a senior at Iona University in New Rochelle. Her mother, Sheila, and I have been divorced for three years.

Fortunately, the divorce has been amicable, and Hannah hasn't suffered too much, at least as far as I can tell. She goes sailing with me every week or so during the summer months, which I'm happy to say has kept us close. She means the world to me.

CHAPTER 3

Seth's office was in downtown White Plains, in a tower across the street from the courthouse. After finding a spot in the parking garage, I rode the elevator to the third floor and entered the reception area. It was tastefully decorated with colorful modern art—not lavish, but reserved. Paula, his assistant, glanced up at me as I entered.

"Good afternoon, Mr. Burnett. I'll let Attorney Bodner know you're here."

"Thanks, Paula."

Paula was an attractive married mother of two and a long-time legal assistant. Seth had chosen an experienced professional to assist him instead of some youthful eye candy fresh out of school. After speaking on the phone momentarily, she rose to usher me into Seth's office.

"Thanks for coming in, Dan. Have a seat." Seth gestured to the sofa in a casual seating cluster. I had not seen him since last November and was reminded of how young and innocent he looked. I knew he was over thirty, but he looked about twenty with straight blond hair and a boyish face; it appeared he did not yet need to shave.

"So, how have you been?" I asked.

Sitting across from me in a wingback chair, wearing a crisp white shirt and deep red patterned tie, he replied, "I'm good."

"How did you land a high-profile case like this?"

"Hey, they wanted the best!" he laughed.

Knowing Seth, I was sure he was joking. He is the least bragga-docious and most unassuming attorney I've ever met. But he just might be the best.

He handed me a file and told me the story.

"According to his parents, Jerome Jordan was driving home around eight p.m. on the evening of March 1 from classes at the SUNY campus in Valhalla. For a bit of background, he comes from a religious, hard-working, middle-class family with a younger sister. He excelled in school and sports. His grades were good enough to receive a full scholarship from SUNY to study biology."

"The officer's statements show he was driving south of Route 287 on North Broadway when they began following in their patrol car. As he approached town, he failed to use a signal, and they attempted to pull him over. They claim Jerome was driving erratically, and they both say he didn't immediately pull over but finally stopped several blocks later. They approached the driver's side, where the window was down, and asked for a license and registration. As Jerome reached into the glove compartment, Officer O'Riley claimed he saw a gun. He then ordered Jerome to put both hands on the wheel. That was when they both said that Jerome mouthed off to them, and Officer Maddox ordered Jerome to get out of the car. They both say Jerome continued to mouth off repeatedly, using curse words. Officer Maddox then opened the door and attempted to pull Jerome out. They both claim that Jerome refused to get out of the car, continued cursing, and appeared to be under the influence of drugs or alcohol. It was then that

Officer O'Riley tased Jerome, and he fell out the door into the street. By the way, you'll see in the report that no gun was found.

"So far, this sounds like how every case of police brutality starts," I said. "Exactly." Seth continued, "They claim they ordered Jerome to remain on the ground, but he tried to get up. Then they struck Jerome with fists and a nightstick about the head, arms, and shoulders. Interestingly, each of the officers claimed the other struck the first blow. They both say that after just a few blows, Jerome became unconscious, and they immediately called for backup and an ambulance."

"You said on the phone that the police refuse to release the bodycam and patrol car footage?"

"That's correct. They claim they're still determining if it's useful."

"You're kidding. That's the lamest excuse I've ever heard."

"They're going to need to release it soon; the public will demand it."

"Agreed," I said, shaking my head in disgust.

"So, I'd like to find some video of our own to see what happened. If it looks bad for the police, I'll release it to the media and force them to refute it. I have a press conference scheduled for 5:00 today and will be offering a reward for any first-hand testimony or cell phone camera images."

"I assume you'd like me to canvass the neighborhood for the same?"

"Exactly. The sooner, the better," Seth replied.

"I can start this afternoon."

"Good. Let me see your terms of engagement."

I handed him the one-page form. He skimmed it quickly, took out a pen, signed it, and handed it back.

"Ask Paula to make a copy on your way out. Good luck!"

After reaching my car, I opened the file Seth had given me. Along with the police report, there were photos of Jerome. They showed a badly bruised face, eyes swollen shut, visible stitches, and missing teeth. Reading the medical report, they listed all the contusions and wounds and noted that his jaw was broken and wired shut. He had a broken arm and broken ribs, which the doctors said were consistent with being kicked. Looking back through the hospital pictures, I saw tubes and wires, bandages, and an arm cast. After thirty years on the police force, I had seen it all before, but still, the images were sickening.

The police report stated the car was stopped along the southbound lane in a divided section of North Broadway near Tibbetts Park. I knew this to be a prosperous, busy downtown area and was only a few blocks from Seth's office.

Leaving the car parked where it was, I walked to Tibbets Park and saw it was in the median between the southbound and northbound lanes. To the west were mainly commercial buildings, and beyond the park to the east were apartment buildings. I walked the west side of the street to see if any establishments would have been open at eight p.m. Sal's Pizza had hours posted to nine p.m. So I went inside and asked a young man behind the counter if he was there the night of March 1. He slid a calendar from under the counter, glanced at it, and said he was not, but said that Cindy and Sal were on that night. He told me Sal would not be back until 5:00 that day but introduced me to Cindy, who was waiting tables. While waiting for her to finish with a customer, I glanced at the surroundings and saw bright fluorescent lighting and a red and white Formica interior with black and white checkerboard floors.

Cindy, an energetic young woman with a ponytail, said she hadn't seen anything until all the police cars and ambulances arrived. She explained that when she looked out, a crowd had gathered and blocked her view of what was happening. I asked if they had any surveillance cameras, and she told me there was one behind the counter aimed at the cash register and another at the door. She added that they recorded for forty-eight hours before re-recording over themselves. When I asked if the police had come in to view them, she said she wasn't aware of it but that I should ask Sal, who was the owner. I thanked her for her time, made a few notes, and continued down the street.

Having seen no other storefronts that would have been open at that hour, I crossed through the park to the east side of the street. While in the park, I noticed two surveillance cameras on light poles. I took a picture of each with my phone and noted their location, thinking we could request the footage from the city.

I entered a Thai restaurant on the east side of North Broadway, at the corner of Main Street. The interior was more inviting than Sal's, with light wood and paper screens between the booths and softer lighting. A copper fountain near the front door provided a relaxing sound of trickling water. I spoke to Mr. Boonmee, who said he was the owner. After asking who I was, I got pretty much the same story from him as from Cindy at the pizza place. He said they were busy that night and didn't notice anything until all the police cars and ambulances arrived with flashing lights and sirens. I asked if they had any cameras, and he told me they did, and a monitoring company retained the footage on the cloud. Asking how I could obtain a copy, he picked up the phone, called the monitoring company, and after exchanging a few words, he handed me the phone. They asked for my email address and told me they would upload a copy for the evening of March 1. I could not have asked for anything more.

The remaining side of the street was apartment buildings. I counted three along that block, all brownstones, across from the park. I went into the first, rang the bell for the super, and he greeted me at the front door. I flashed my license and asked if he had seen anything. He told me he had not, but Ms. Cooper, in 307, told him she had seen the whole thing and felt sorry for the young man.

When I asked if she was home, he said I was welcome to check.

I rode a tired elevator to the third floor and knocked on the door of 307.

While waiting in the hall, I noticed the unpleasant scent of cooked cabbage. The hall was dingy and poorly lit, and the carpet was well-worn. After a half-minute, the door opened a few inches, limited by a chain.

"Ms. Cooper?" I asked. "Yes, who are you?"

I showed her my I.D. and said, "I'm sorry to bother you, but I was told you saw what happened on the street last Friday night?"

When she opened the door, I saw a thirty-ish Black woman who spoke softly, "I did. It was just horrid what the police did to that young man."

"What did you see, Ma'am?"

"They beat and kicked him mercilessly. I can't believe they didn't kill him. I see on the news they came pretty close."

"Might you have taken any pictures?"

"No, I didn't think of it until it was all over."

"Would you be willing to make a statement about what you witnessed?"

"I can't get involved. The last thing I need is to have the police on my case. I'm trying to raise two small children here, and I don't need any trouble."

"The Jordan family is offering a reward for any information. I'll see that you get some of it if you make a statement,"

"How much?"

"A thousand dollars."

"Oh, we could use that. Let me talk to my husband about it; do you have a card?"

I handed her one of my cards and told her to watch the evening news tonight after 5:00. "The Jordan family and their attorney will hold a press conference and discuss the reward."

I heard some youthful commotion inside her apartment, and she said she'd let me know, then closed the door. While riding down the elevator, I thought her eyewitness testimony could be valuable. It's not as good as a video, but with other eyewitness corroboration, it could help make a case against the cops.

After exiting the building, I checked the time and saw it was nearly 4:00. Wanting to return to Mia's to watch the press conference, I retrieved my car and headed to Mamaroneck. On the way, with my phone in a holder on the dash, I called Seth and told him about Ms. Cooper and the cameras in the park. He sounded pleased with my progress and said he would talk with me in the morning. Next, I called Mia and told her I was on my way.

CHAPTER 4

Arriving at Mia's, I parked in the circle by the front door she had left unlocked for me. I found her watching the news in the TV room open to the kitchen on a big- screen television mounted on a wall adjacent to a stone fireplace. After a quick kiss and hello, I stood behind her seat and watched as the image on the screen showed a massive mob in front of the White Plains Police Department, holding signs and demanding the release of the bodycam footage. The camera focused on a podium where the police made their statements while the commentators told us that Jerome Jordan's attorney would address the crowd any minute now.

A few minutes after 5:00, Seth stepped up to the podium. Behind him, signs read Justice for Jerome, End Police Brutality, Hands-Up-Don't-Shoot, and a few others. When Seth tapped the microphone, the crowd quieted just enough to hear him speak.

"Good afternoon, everyone. My name is Seth Bodner; the Jordan family has asked me to represent Jerome. Right now, he remains unconscious in the intensive care unit at White Plains Hospital. I'm here to announce a ten- thousand-dollar reward the Jordan family is offering for any information or video images of this senseless attack."

He provided a link to a GoFundMe page where anyone could donate to increase the reward. He then addressed the White Plains Police Department's uncooperative behavior.

"So far, the police are the only ones who know what occurred that night. Jerome is unable to speak for himself. Perhaps they hope Jerome will die and the truth will never be told. We are demanding they release the video from the patrol car and the bodycams from officers O'Riley and Maddox. Only then will we know what happened. That concludes my statement, but I'm prepared to take questions."

All the reporters yelled their questions at once. A moderator with the microphone chose who would be heard. The first up was from 1010 WINS radio.

"Why won't the WPPD release the video?"

Seth replied, "I can only speculate, but I would assume it is damning evidence of police brutality."

Next was NBC New York. "Aren't there laws requiring the police to release the video to the tax-paying public?"

"That is up to the Attorney General. I assume he has reviewed the video by now; he's the one keeping it from you," Seth replied.

"Was this attack racially motivated?" Someone else asked. The crowd became increasingly agitated after every question.

"I can't say for sure at this time. As we all know, Jerome is Black, and both police officers are white."

After a few more questions and hostility from the crowd, Seth thanked everyone for coming, stepped away from the podium, and disappeared from the cameras. As the news commentator reiterated what we had all seen, the crowd dispersed, and the station went to commercial.

"How do you feel about all this?" Mia asked.

"It's complicated. Let me make us a cocktail, and I'll try to put my feelings into words."

I took a few steps into the kitchen, removed a cocktail shaker from the cabinet, filled it most of the way with ice, and poured a healthy amount of Elijah Craig bourbon and a splash of sweet vermouth. After shaking it well, I took two martini glasses from the glass door cabinet and dropped in a couple of burgundy cherries. After a few final shakes, I strained the contents into the glasses and served one to Mia. I took the other, sat down beside her, and after savoring the first sip, I answered her question.

"I've seen the hospital pictures of Jerome and read the doctor's reports. It is absolutely awful what those cops did to him. I hope he makes it, but he might not. However, I'll have to choose between standing up for fellow cops and continuing this investigation. There is an unwritten rule in police work to always protect the department. It's called 'The Blue Wall of Silence.'"

"Could there be any other explanation for his wounds?" Mia asked.

"I can't imagine one. I don't know if Jerome did anything to provoke the police officers to the point they feared for their safety. Outside of that, their job is to serve and protect."

"I understand your conflict, Dan. But now that you're no longer with the department, don't you feel free to do the right thing, whatever that is?"

"I don't know. Thirty years with the department weighs pretty heavily on me. I'll have to wrestle with this for a day or two."

She hugged me and said, "I'm sure you'll make the right decision, love." After looking into my eyes to sense my emotions, she said, "I brought home some yellowfin tuna for dinner. When would you like to eat?"

"Soon, if it's okay with you, I'm hungry."

"I'll start prepping now. It should be ready in half an hour or so."

"Sounds good; I'm going to hop in the shower."

I always found the shower a good place to think. As the steaming water beat down on my shoulders, I relived the day's events. I reflected on my time with the department and thought about how I would have reacted if I were still on the force. I probably would have assumed Jerome deserved it and not given it another thought. But now, all I could think about were the pictures I had seen of him in the hospital—a haunting image.

After washing my hair, I sensed Mia entering the bathroom; a moment later, she stepped into the shower naked and started washing my body with soap. It wasn't long before she reached areas that aroused me.

"I thought you might need some help relaxing," she whispered.

One thing led to another, and we ended up in bed, where she had already turned down the covers. After some pretty intense lovemaking, she whispered, "I hope you didn't mind delaying dinner a bit."

"Never." I laughed before kissing her again.

We sat down to plates of sesame-crusted seared rare tuna with a reduced soy- ginger glaze and steamed bok choy. She's a fantastic cook, and other than a few oohs and aahs from me, we remained silent while enjoying each bite. We stayed at the table, sipping Pinot Gris when our plates were clean.

"Would you like to talk more about your conflicts?" she asked.

"Not really; I thought I'd learn more about the two cops before making a decision."

"That makes sense," she nodded.

"Would you excuse me while I make a phone call? I'll help clean up when I'm done."

"No problem, love," she said.

I called Sal's Pizza restaurant from the living room while looking out at the lights on the water. A male voice answered.

"Is this Sal?" I inquired.

"You got him."

"My name is Dan Burnett. I was in earlier today and spoke to Cindy about the incident outside your restaurant last Friday night. She told me you were there, too."

"Yes. There were cops and ambulances all over the place."

"The Jordan Family's attorney has hired me to investigate. Is there anything you can tell me that might be useful?"

"Hold on a sec," he said, as I heard him taking payment from a customer. When he picked up the phone again, he said, "I went outside for a look after all the flashing lights were there. All I saw was the young man propped up against the front tire—he appeared to be dead. A bunch of cops and EMTs were standing over him."

"Would you be willing to make a statement to that effect? There's reward money available."

"Sure, I'm surprised the police have not already been in asking questions."

"Great. Will you be in tomorrow?"

"From noon to closing."

"Okay, I'll stop by tomorrow afternoon. Thanks again, Sal."

After hanging up, I jotted down some notes to share with Seth in the morning and rejoined Mia in the kitchen. The table was clear, the dishes were done, and she poured each of us a small glass of Port.

"Shall we take these into the living room?" she asked. "That sounds wonderful."

We cuddled on the couch, watching the lights and the stars over the Sound. This was our happy place, where we were most content. It wasn't long before I heard some faint snoring from her, but we remained in each other's arms for a while before I guided her up the stairs and into bed. After climbing into bed myself, she rolled over, snuggled into me, and we slept soundly through the night.

CHAPTER 5

"Did you see the press conference?" Seth asked.

"I did. Did you have any luck with the park cameras?"

"Not yet. I reached the parks department yesterday afternoon, but they told me they couldn't release any footage without permission from the Mayor's office. I'll be calling him shortly."

Sitting at the kitchen table, halfway through my first coffee of the day, I told him about my discussion with Sal last night and his willingness to make a statement, then asked how he would like to handle that.

"I'd like him to come into my office, where I can arrange for a stenographer and video camera to record his statement. I can also send a car to drive him to and from the office."

"Your office is only three blocks from Tibbets Park. How about I just escort him there?"

"Even better."

"Okay, Sal told me he'll be in after noon today. I can stop by and speak with him about that and go back to the apartment buildings to post some notices of the reward and see if I can find anyone who might have seen anything."

"Perfect. If I compose an offer of reward and email it to you, can you print some out?" Seth offered.

"Sure, no problem."

"Great, I'll get that to you within the hour."

"Okay. I'll let you know how it goes."

I took a second cup of coffee into the dining room with my laptop and checked emails. There was one from the Boonmee Restaurant's security company with a file attached. When I started to review the video, there was a timestamp of noon on March 1. I fast-forwarded to 7:50 and began watching. At 8:02, the police cruiser with lights flashing pulled in behind an older Honda Accord. The view was from the restaurant's front door, and the detail from across the park was dark and grainy. I was able to zoom in, but the more I zoomed, the picture quality deteriorated. The shrubbery in the park blocked the view of anything within three feet from the ground, but I was able to see Jerome step from the car, put his hands on the roof, and then Officer Maddox take his hands behind him and place handcuffs on his wrists. The foliage obscured anything below that. A moment later, I saw Officer O'Riley strike Jerome on the side of his head with a nightstick. After the second blow, Jerome hunched over to protect himself, and I saw Officer Maddox swinging his bare fists, striking Jerome in the head multiple times.

Within moments, Jerome disappeared from view behind the shrubbery, but it appeared that both officers continued striking down, I assume at Jerome. Considering that this camera was set up to record what was happening within twenty feet, to be able to see what was happening over two hundred feet away was a stretch. What was indisputable, though, was that the beating began after Jerome was cuffed. I rewound the video, noted the time of the first blow, and then let it play.

They had been raining blows on Jerome for one minute and twenty seconds before Officer Maddox returned to the patrol car and opened the door. From this view, what he was doing wasn't clear, but I assumed he was calling for assistance. Within a minute, an additional police car arrived, followed by an ambulance. There was no further violence after that point in time.

I continued watching until the medical personnel placed Jerome on a stretcher, loaded him in the ambulance, and drove off. The total elapsed time from when Jerome pulled over to the ambulance leaving the scene was twenty- six minutes. Most of that time, it was just police and paramedics standing around. From this camera's distant view and grainy image, it could not be seen if anyone was administering medical assistance.

I immediately forwarded this email and attachment to Seth and opened his email with the reward notice. After a quick look, I sent it to Mia's printer in the home office on the other side of the foyer. Once finished with the rest of my emails, I closed my laptop, retrieved a half-dozen printed notices, and prepared to leave. After gathering my things, I kissed Mia and headed to White Plains.

While on the road, I remembered that I had made plans with Hannah for dinner that night and called her.

"Hi, Dad."

"Good morning, Han. Are we still on for dinner tonight?"

"I'm looking forward to it," she replied.

"What are you hungry for?"

"How about Giuseppe's?

"Sounds good! We haven't been in a while."

"Does 6:00 work for you?"

"Yup, I'll pick you up then."

"Bye, Dad."

After ending the call, I wondered if it was time to tell Hannah about Mia. I had been putting it off for months and knew I shouldn't have let it go this long. I guess I was afraid of disappointing her if she had any visions of me and her mom getting back together. We had never discussed that possibility, but I thought that's what most kids wish for. Anxiety hit me in the gut when I decided that now was the time to tell her. I took a few deep breaths and tried to relax and enjoy the beautiful sunny day on the road with light traffic. A few minutes later, Seth called.

"That's decent footage, Dan. Even though it's not very clear, it confirms my suspicion of how it went down," he exclaimed.

"I thought it might. If I can get Sal in today, can you depose him?"

"With a couple of hours' notice, I can."

"I'm heading to White Plains now. I plan to speak with Ms. Cooper and see if she is willing to come in, too."

"It would be good if we could do them one after the other while I have the staff here."

"I'll see what she says. She's afraid of the police."

"I understand. I'll talk to you soon."

I found a parking spot near Tibbets Park and entered the apartment building where Ms. Cooper lives. I rang her bell, and after identifying myself, she buzzed me in. I stopped at a bulletin board by the mailboxes, posted the reward notice, and headed up the stairs. Upon reaching her door, I saw she had left it partially open for me, and after knocking lightly, I entered her apartment and called her name.

I heard, "Come on in, Mr. Burnett. I'm just changing a diaper; I'll be with you in a minute."

"No rush."

A minute later, she appeared carrying a baby girl. If my distant memories of my own life were accurate, I guessed she was nearly a year old and about ready to start walking. Ms. Cooper gestured to a chair in her living room, sat on the adjacent sofa, and fed her baby from a bottle. She seemed a bit harried from juggling small children.

"Have you spoken to your husband about making a statement, Ms. Cooper?"

"I have, and please call me Rose. Ms. Cooper sounds like my mother."

"That's fine, Rose. You can call me Dan. How old is your little girl?"

"Eleven months. She's getting to be a handful."

"I can remember that well—getting into everything."

"That's for sure; I can't leave her alone for a second."

After a brief pause, she said, "Tell me more about the reward money."

"The Jordan Family has put up ten thousand dollars for information or evidence that shows what happened that night. Their attorney is offering a minimum of one thousand of that money to anyone who comes forward and up to the whole ten if the information is overwhelming."

"We could really use the money, Dan. Will my name be on the news?"

"Only if you want it to be; I can understand your privacy concern. We can keep it out of the media, and the only time it would be on the record is if you testify in court someday, which is unlikely."

"Okay, I'll do it."

"Great. Jerome's family will be very appreciative. Would any time today be convenient?"

"Well, my son will be home from kindergarten at noon. Could we do it some morning, when I'll just have this little one?"

"How about tomorrow? I'm sure you could bring her; the attorney's office is just a few blocks away. What time would be best?"

"Any time after 9:00. So long as I'm back before noon."

"Okay, I'll set it up and have a car service drive you and your baby."

"Oh no. I don't want anyone to see me getting into a chauffeur-driven car."

"How about if I walk with you? Do you have a stroller?"

"I do. That will be fine."

"Great. May I have your phone number so I can confirm a time with you?"

I entered the number into my phone, thanked her, and promised to call later that day.

When I returned to the street, it was still before noon. I walked to the rest of the apartment buildings in the area to post the reward notices. In each case, I rang the super to let me in. They were all cooperative except the Westchester Arms. He would not allow anything to be posted in the lobby.

When finished, I walked across the street to the pizza place. Sal was behind the register, and he appeared precisely like I had imagined from our phone conversation: A thin, dark-haired, Italian-looking man in his thirties wearing a white double-breasted chef's coat. Even though it was only noon, he already had a five o'clock shadow.

After introducing myself and shaking hands, I asked if any time today would be good to walk to Seth's office to make his statement.

"I only have one other person on this afternoon until 5:00 when we get real busy. How about around lunchtime tomorrow? I can put an extra person on to cover for me."

"Great, shall we say noon?"

"Okay, I'll see you then."

I stepped out on the sidewalk feeling disappointed that I couldn't deliver either of them to Seth that day. Not seeing anything more I could do, I crossed the street and returned to my car, opening the window to let some heat escape from the sun-soaked interior. I called Mia to explain why I wouldn't be home for dinner that night. As always, she was supportive of me spending time with Hannah. Next, I called Seth to tell him his morning tomorrow was booked.

"That's good, Dan. With a couple of statements and the video from the Thai place, I should have enough to go to the media."

"Any luck with the mayor's office?"

"Not yet. They say they'll look at the footage, see if anything is useful, and get back to me."

"Useful to who?"

"Exactly."

"Any news on Jerome?"

"They've removed the ventilator, and he's breathing on his own but still unconscious, so I guess that's progress."

"Good to hear. What time would you like Rose Cooper to arrive?"

"Let's shoot for 10:00."

"Okay, I'll bring her by then. So that you know, she'll be bringing her eleven-month-old daughter with her."

"Not a problem. Paula will keep her occupied. See you then."

Still having the afternoon to kill before dinner with Hannah, I headed to the marina to check on Privateer.

CHAPTER 6

When I arrived, there were a few other people on the docks. The nice day had brought them out like it had me. The marina had five finger docks connected by one long floating dock along the shore. This was accessed by a ramp that went up and down with the tide.

My boat's name is "Privateer." She was ten years old when I bought her, getting a great deal from the seized property department of the State of New York. I participated in that seizure as the arresting officer after catching three guys smuggling drugs into New York Harbor from the Bahamas. That was six years ago. I had always dreamed of owning a sailboat like that and teaching Hannah to sail. As a teenager, I sailed dinghies on Long Island Sound and hoped that Hannah would enjoy it as I had. However, this boat was much larger: a forty-three-foot Tartan sloop with two staterooms, a head, and a full galley.

Other than needing a good wash, Privateer was in fine shape. Going below, it didn't smell too bad, considering she had been closed up all winter. The batteries were fully charged, and everything worked when I turned on the electronics—Hallelujah! I opened the floorboards and tested the bilge pump; it also worked. After connecting the cable TV, I took out a notebook and started a list of all the work needed before leaving the dock. There was plenty of time, but I liked to have an organized plan. I spent the afternoon inspecting things and adding to the list. At the top of the list was hiring a diver to clean the bottom.

After sitting motionless for five months in Long Island Sound, there would definitely be a coating of algae, if not barnacles, below the waterline.

At 5:30, I left to pick up Hannah at Iona University, just a few exits east on I-95. She was waiting in front of her dorm and effortlessly ran to the car, wearing jeans and a hoodie. Hannah is tall—five-ten, thin, and athletic, with long sandy blonde hair. She gave me a peck on the cheek as she entered the car.

"Have you already decided what you're having tonight?" she asked.

"I'm thinking linguini with red clam sauce. How about you?"

"You know I love Giuseppe's lasagna. I've been thinking about it all day," she added, "and their garlic bread!"

Giuseppe's was a little family place we had been going to since Hannah was a child. His wife, Bianca, waited tables and always fussed over Hannah as she grew up. As we walked toward the front door, the aroma of garlic filled the air. When we entered, Bianca rushed over to welcome us. As always, she wore a black waitress uniform and apron, her hair tied up in a bun.

"Hannah!" she exclaimed. "It's been so long since I've seen you; you're a full-grown woman now. And so pretty; I'll bet you're driving the boys mad!"

Hannah blushed and said, "Not now, Bianca. I'm with my Dad!"

"I can see that. Good evening, Mr. Burnett."

"Good evening, Bianca. It's good to see you."

"Let's have you sit by the front window, your favorite table."

"Thank you. How about we start with a bottle of Chianti?"

"Coming right up," she said before scurrying away.

Hannah and I looked at each other and laughed. Although older, Bianca hadn't changed much in all the years we had been coming here. The interior of the restaurant hadn't changed either. On one wall was a mural of the Bay of Naples with Mount Vesuvius in the background, and on another wall, there were shelves with Chianti bottles in wicker baskets. Bianca returned with the wine and a basket of garlic bread. After she had opened the bottle and filled our glasses, we gave her our order without opening a menu. Once again, she scurried to the kitchen to give Giuseppe our order.

Bianca was right; Hannah was pretty. While I'm sure every father thinks their daughter is beautiful, Hannah was especially so. I have always noticed how people look at her; she has crystal blue eyes that grab your attention, and her little button nose as a child has become perfect over time. Even so, she never seems to be obsessed with her looks.

After we each had a sip of wine, I said, "There is something I have been meaning to discuss with you, Han. I've been seeing a woman, and it's becoming serious."

"Thanks for telling me. I've suspected that for a while and am happy for you. I'd hate to think you would spend the rest of your life alone."

"I was afraid you'd be disappointed that your Mom and I wouldn't get back together."

"Well, I used to hope for that, but after seeing no sparks between you last Thanksgiving, I knew it wouldn't happen. I'm fine with that."

"Was I that transparent?"

"Only to me. Mom wanted to leave the door open for you, but I know you too well. It's okay. What's her name?"

"Mia Davis. Her brother was the lawyer whose body was found in the trunk of a car a couple of years ago."

"Was she your client?"

"Yes, but we didn't become romantic until it was over."

"No need to explain, Dad; I'm not judging anyone here. When do I get to meet her?"

"I hoped she could join us on the boat sometime."

"I'd like that. Please know I'm happy for you."

We each picked up a piece of garlic bread and took a bite. After a moment, I said, "You're so mature, Han. Thank you for that."

She reached for my hand and squeezed it momentarily, then took a sip of wine. Bianca returned from the kitchen with our entrées and then went to another table to take their order. While enjoying our meals, our conversation progressed to the boat and sailing. I was relieved to have the Mia discussion behind me.

Later, when I returned to Mia's house, she was lying on the living room couch, reading a book with her head on a pillow. A crescent moon was just above the horizon in the night sky. I leaned over the back and kissed her on the forehead.

"How was your dinner with Hannah?" she asked.

"Very nice. I finally found the courage to tell her about you."

"How did she react?"

"She was happy for me. She said she had suspected there was someone in my life for a while. We had a very mature conversation, and she wants to meet you."

"Really? I'd like that, too."

"I told her we will do it on the boat sometime; we'll go for a sail."

"Sounds wonderful; I'm dying for you to take me sailing," she said.

"Would you like a tot of port?"

"Yes, if you join me and enjoy this clear night sky."

I went to the little bar counter in the kitchen, poured us two small glasses, and joined her on the couch. She lifted her legs for me to sit, then stretched them out again on my lap.

"How was your day?" she asked.

With a sigh, I said, "Quite productive. I obtained some camera footage from a restaurant that showed most of the incident. I also arranged for two eyewitness statements for Seth to take tomorrow. Together, that will give him something to work with. He'll probably hold another press conference to ratchet up the pressure on City Hall."

"And how are you feeling about your loyalty to the Department?"

"Still conflicted. However, after seeing the video today, I'll have difficulty walking away from this case."

She reached out and caressed my cheek, and then we returned our gaze to the night sky. We remained there until we had finished our port, then made our way upstairs hand in hand.

CHAPTER 7

I was up and out of the house at 8:30 the following morning. On my way to White Plains, I called my partner, Jim Abbott, also a former NYPD detective.

"Good morning, Dan," he answered.

"Good morning. Will you be in the office this afternoon?"

"Yup."

"I want to tell you about a case I'm working on. I'm thinking around 1:00?"

"See you then, buddy."

When I arrived at Rose Cooper's apartment building, she buzzed me in. After knocking on her door, she opened it wearing makeup and a nice dress. Her hair was stacked on her head, revealing colorful earrings, and I saw a stroller parked in the living room.

"Good morning, Rose. You look lovely today!"

"Thanks, Dan. I'm a bit nervous."

"Nothing to be worried about. Attorney Bodner is a nice guy, and his assistant, Paula, is looking forward to meeting your daughter. What's her name, by the way?"

"Ayo, it's short for Ayodele."

"What a lovely name."

"Thank you. I'll get her ready, and we can go. Make yourself comfortable."

I sat in a chair by the door, took out my phone, and scanned through the messages. Within a few minutes, Rose reappeared with Ayo in her arms. She wore a pink ruffly dress and a matching ribbon in her curly dark hair. I recalled Hannah in a dress like that twenty years ago. Rose put a coat on her daughter, placed her in the stroller, and said, "Shall we?"

We rode the elevator to the ground floor and exited the building. After crossing both lanes, Rose pointed out where the beating occurred. Nodding, I thanked her for pointing that out, even though I already knew. There was still a hint of spring in the air, with a clear blue sky, but the wind had picked up, making it feel colder than it actually was. Rose paused to bundle up her daughter, and we continued three more blocks to Seth's office.

After riding the elevator to the third floor, we entered the warm office and were greeted by Paula. "Good morning, Ms. Cooper. I've been looking forward to meeting this little one," she exclaimed, leaning over and looking into the stroller. "She is just precious!"

"Paula, meet Ayodele," I said. "I call her Ayo," Rose offered.

"That's what I'll call her then. I'll tell Mr. Bodner that you're all here."

She knocked, then opened the inner door to Seth's office. After a moment, she ushered all of us in. After Seth introduced himself and the stenographer, Rose leaned into the stroller and said a few words to Ayo. Then Paula and I wheeled the child out. Paula picked her up and walked her around the office to look at the colorful paintings on the walls. Ayo never fussed once, seeming to enjoy Paula's attention. Seth's door opened forty-five minutes later, and he walked Rose out. They both were smiling.

After Paula placed Ayo in the stroller and said goodbye, the three of us left the office, rode down in the elevator, and I pushed the stroller back to her apartment.

"That was easier than I thought it would be," Rose said.

"Good to hear. I knew there was nothing to be afraid of. Did he give you the reward check?"

"Yes, one thousand dollars, and all I had to do was tell him what I saw. I was afraid he would question me like the lawyers do on TV, but he was very friendly, and I wasn't even aware there was a camera on."

I walked with them until we were inside the lobby, thanked her for making the statement, and said goodbye. I wandered across the street to Sal's a few minutes before noon.

"Hi, Sal."

"Do you want a slice before we go? It's on the house."

"Sure," I replied.

Sal took two slices from behind the glass, put them on paper plates, and set them on a table. He gestured for me to sit, then sat across from me and took a bite. We made small talk while eating, and when we were done, I complimented him on the pizza, and we headed out the door. When we arrived at Seth's, I introduced him to Paula and said, "I trust you can find your way back?"

"No problem," he laughed.

I asked Paula to have Seth call me when he was finished and said goodbye before leaving.

Just before reaching the office in Scarsdale, Seth called. "How did it go?" I asked.

"Very well. They were both credible witnesses. Between their statements and the video from Boonmee, I'll set up a press conference for late this afternoon. I'd like to get it on the evening news."

"I told Ms. Cooper and Sal you would keep their names out of it for now.

Neither of them wants to invite retaliation from the police."

"Of course. After this airs on the news tonight, I'll have grounds to subpoena all the video from WPPD and the park cameras. I'll work on that tonight and file it in the morning. The shit is about to hit the fan at City Hall!"

"As it should. Do you have another minute?"

"Sure."

"I'm having some reservations about going against the police on this. As you know, I was NYPD for thirty years. We had an unwritten rule about siding with the Department and our fellow cops."

"I know about the blue wall of silence, Dan. How would you like to proceed?"

"I'm not sure; I'm still grappling with it. It sounds like these cops were totally out of line here, but I'd like to back off until I learn more about what happened."

"I understand. You've accomplished a lot already. Let's keep in touch for the time being."

"Okay. Thanks for understanding."

"No worries. Send me a bill for your time so far."

"Will do."

After ending the call, I let out a deep sigh. I was temporarily off the hook, but that didn't help with my conscience. I hoped Jim could help me figure it out.

When I entered the office door, Jim stood to greet me, and we gave each other a quick bro-hug. He is tall and thin like me, a couple of years older, but healthy and fit, with curly reddish hair and freckles.

"How have you been, partner?" I asked. "All good. What have you been up to?"

"Let's have a coffee, and I'll tell you about it."

Our office was just one big room with two desks, a conference table, and a cluster of comfortable seating. We also had our own bathroom and a closet along the back wall.

I poured each of us a cup, added the condiments, and carried them to our comfortable seating cluster. We both sat and took a sip, and then I told him, "I've been working on the Jerome Jordan case for Seth Bodner."

He released a descending-tone whistle, then said, "And you're wrestling with going against the police department." He said it as a fact, not a question. "Exactly. I've seen a video and heard statements of what occurred. It will be released to the media tonight, and it looks bad for the police department."

"I saw the attorney on TV a couple of nights ago, and I've seen the pictures of Jerome's face from the hospital. Was it justified?"

"I can't imagine how. They beat him half to death after he was cuffed; maybe to death, time will tell."

"There have always been a few cops that take it too far. Some bad apples use their badge to take out their rage on others. Is there a racist element to this?"

"I'm not sure. But you never hear about a white kid taking a beating like that."

"No. I can recall, not so long ago, some cops calling Black men savages."

"Among other things," I added.

"Times are changing, but maybe not fast enough."

"What would you do if you were me?"

After reflecting momentarily, he said, "I think I'd find out if these guys are outliers. If they have a history of this shit, they need to be held accountable. It shines badly on police everywhere."

We remained silent for a minute to weigh our conversation. Then I said, "Thanks for your thoughts. I think that was where I was heading."

"Good luck with your decision. Let me know if I can help."

"And what have you been working on lately?"

"Ever since we solved that collector car case, the insurance company has been throwing work my way, looking for fraud. Some collectors have also been hiring me to research the history of individual cars before making a purchase."

"Interesting. Should we advertise to that community somehow?"

"Maybe. But right now, there's enough work for both of us," Jim said.

"Wow. That happened fast."

"Yeah, let me know when you can take on a case."

We finished our coffee, and I took the cups to the sink and rinsed them out as Jim returned to his desk. I texted Seth that I would be watching his press conference tonight and asked him to forward any information he could round up on officers O'Riley and Maddox. I thanked Jim again and headed out the door.

Having chosen to take the rest of the day off, I drove back to Mia's, hoping she would join me for a walk on the beach. When I entered the house through the garage, she was in the kitchen chopping vegetables.

"Hi, sweetheart," I said, hugging her from behind with my arms around her waist, inhaling the scent of her hair.

"Hello, love. You're home early."

"I was hoping you'd want to walk on the beach with me."

"I'd love to. Give me a few minutes to finish up."

"Take your time. I need to check emails."

I opened my laptop at the dining room table and returned a few messages. The rest were junk, and I finished quickly. When I returned to the kitchen, Mia was already putting on her sneakers. We headed out the door wearing warm jackets, and she wore a ski hat. After a one-block downhill walk, we reached the beach and headed west, holding hands, with the sun and the wind in our faces. We glanced up at her house, setting majestically on the hill.

"So, how was your day, sweetheart?" I asked.

"Not bad. I met a friend downtown at the farmers market, and we went for coffee. She wanted to talk to me about her troubles with her husband."

"What kind of troubles?"

"She thinks he's becoming an alcoholic."

"Oh. What did you tell her?"

"Well, we talked about AA and other similar programs. Thankfully, he's never violent."

Sensing Mia's concern, I asked, "How much does he drink?"

"She says he starts as soon as he gets home and has a half dozen every night, often passing out after dinner."

"That would certainly qualify as an alcoholic."

"I know how easily it can become a habit. My Mom, god rest her soul, had issues with alcohol. Judy and I had to do an intervention to get her to face the problem and seek help. You've probably noticed that I limit myself to two drinks a day?"

"I have noticed that but never thought much about it."

"That's the reason. They say alcohol addiction runs in the family, so I watch it closely."

"I had no idea. I wish I had the opportunity to meet your Mom."

"Well, she passed a dozen years ago, but she would have loved you."

"I guess I'll have to take your word for it."

"You can trust me on that. So tell me about your day."

I told her about my discussions with Seth and Jim and my decision to back off the case until I learned more. I also told her about Seth's media plan for this afternoon. After about a mile, when our hands and faces became cold, we turned around with the wind at our backs and quickly returned to her house.

She put a tea kettle on the stove while I turned on the local news. I guess Seth had released the video because every station was playing it on a continuous loop, with commentators calling it police brutality and Black leaders calling it a racial hate crime. We were told that the

Jordan family's attorney would speak in front of City Hall at 5:30. That was nearly an hour from now, but the cameras were already set up and showed an angry mob forming. Mia carried over our hot tea and sat beside me, engrossed by what we were watching.

A few minutes later, she rose to prepare dinner, explaining that she was making vegetable beef soup and it would need to cook a while. I remained in front of the TV, enjoying the aroma of meat and onions browning on the stove. When she added the vegetables and broth, she sat down beside me again while it simmered.

Soon, the picture returned to the scene at City Hall, this time with the Mayor at the podium. After a few moments, he read a prepared statement declaring that the City took police conduct very seriously and that the two officers had been placed on paid leave. He also said the Chief of Police would make a statement after Attorney Bodner. The crowd was getting restless as we watched Seth approach the podium to address them.

"For the last five days, I have asked the City to release the patrol car and bodycam videos, and they have so far refused. Today, we saw why. I released security camera footage that showed Jerome Jordan being beaten mercilessly by the two police officers after he was in hand-cuffs. Clearly, by this time, Jerome was not a threat to the safety of the officers. Instead of defusing the situation, as police procedure calls for, they brutally beat the young man nearly to death.

Jerome has yet to regain consciousness, and if he dies, these officers should be charged with murder."

He paused to let the crowd erupt. Before they became violent, Seth motioned for quiet. He clearly showed skill in leading a crowd.

Seth continued, "Other than the video you all saw today, two eyewitness statements were taken under oath with a court stenographer. These accounts are consistent with what the video shows. Once again, I call for the city to release the bodycam and patrol car video, along with the video from the Tibbets Park surveillance cameras. I will be filing subpoenas for them when the court opens tomorrow morning. The Jordan family deserves justice. The people of New York deserve Justice."

He left the podium without taking questions, leaving the Chief of Police to deal with the crowd. It wasn't long before a chant started from the crowd: "We want the truth; we want the truth; we want the truth." Over and over, they chanted while the Chief of Police tried to calm the crowd. Eventually, they quieted as he spoke.

"Over the last few days, we have analyzed the available video with the Attorney General. Today, as the Mayor told you, we placed Officers O'Riley and Maddox on leave pending further investigation. It is the Attorney General's responsibility to release the video. I have spoken with him and recommended that he do so. I have time for a few questions."

Most of the media had microphones already on the podium. Those who didn't jammed them in his face. He stepped back slightly to avoid injury while the reporters yelled their questions. Most of them were, *"Why did you wait so long?"* Or, *"Do these cops have a history of violence?"* And, *"When will we see the bodycams?"*

This went on for ten minutes, with basically the same questions asked in different ways. Eventually, the Mayor returned to the podium, thanked the crowd, thanked the Chief, and led him away. After more chanting by the crowd, the station broke away to a panel of commentators to tell us what we had just seen and to condemn the Police Department.

At the next commercial, Mia rose to check on the soup. I had been taken in by what I had seen on TV and felt pretty amped up. Attempting to calm down, I shut off the TV and opened a bottle of Cabernet. I poured us each a glass while she stirred some seasonings into the soup. We sat at the kitchen table tucked in a bay window overlooking the beach we had just walked, watching the orange ribbons of sunset over the Manhattan skyline. As we touched glasses and took our first sip, I commented, "That was quite a scene."

"I'll say. Did the Police really think this would all blow over?"

"Maybe they hoped it would. Seth is pretty good, eh?"

"That's for sure. He had the crowd eating out of his hand."

We remained at the table chatting for a while until Mia served dinner. She sliced a fresh baguette to accompany the soup. Everything she makes is wonderful. When her husband was alive, they vacationed at European cooking schools, and she applied what she learned whenever possible. I had gained five pounds since moving in with her.

After cleaning up after dinner, we enjoyed a quiet evening in the living room in front of the glass doors overlooking Long Island Sound. This was our happy place, where we relaxed in front of a starry night sky.

CHAPTER 8

Officer Sean O'Riley

At 9:00 sharp, when Sean O'Riley and John Maddox walked into the Police Conduct Review hearing, Police Captain James Johnson pulled Officer O'Riley into a side conference room and closed the door. "Listen, Sean, the civilians on this oversight board are a bunch of liberal mother fuckers out to get you. Do not admit to anything, and place blame on your rookie partner wherever possible. Got it?"

"Got it, Cap."

"Captain Owens and I will do our damnedest to show you in the best possible light, but quite frankly, your record will work against you. We'll try to gloss over it if they go down that path, but there may be little we can do."

"I appreciate it, Cap."

"And you better hope the Jordan kid doesn't die, or there will be nothing we can do to save you."

O'Riley said nothing; he just nodded.

"Okay, Sean, good luck, and listen to your union rep. He's on your side," Johnson said as he opened the door, and they returned to the hallway.

O'Riley found the bench where the union rep and his partner, Officer Maddox, were seated and joined them. O'Riley was in a uniform that fit snugly over his weight-lifter's upper body and had a completely shaved head. Maddox, also in uniform, had a thinner, youthful stature and a full head of dark hair and mustache. A few minutes later, when the review board was all in place, they were motioned to enter the hearing room. The review board was seated at a long table and consisted of three civilians, along with Chief Allen, Captains Johnson and Owens, and an attorney representing the city, Marshall Green.

O'Riley, Maddox, and their union rep, Jim McCarthy, sat at another table facing forward. When everyone was seated, Howard King, the civilian chair of the oversight board, led the hearing.

"I assume everyone here has seen the patrol car and bodycam video?"

Everyone at the front table nodded. Jim McCarthy said, "Yes, I've reviewed it with the Officers involved."

"Mr. McCarthy, do either of the Officers have an explanation for why standard police procedures were not followed?"

McCarthy nodded to O'Riley, indicating it was his opportunity to speak. "We both thought Mr. Jordan was under the influence of drugs and feared for our safety."

King asked, "What did the toxicology report show?"

Captain Johnson, reading from the report, stated, "There was no indication of drugs or alcohol in the sample taken."

"Officer Maddox, did you think Mr. Jordan was a threat to your safety?"

"I'm not sure, Sir. I'm a rookie and was following my partner's lead."

"How about after he was handcuffed; was he a threat to your safety then?" asked King.

"No, Sir."

"Yet it was after he was handcuffed that you began beating him. Why was that?"

"I have no answer, Sir," Maddox replied. "Do you have an answer, Officer O'Riley?"

"No, Sir."

"Does anyone else on the committee have a question or comment?" King asked.

Captain Owens said, "I would like to state for the record that these two men are both fine officers and an asset to the community."

"Judging from Officer O'Riley's service history, Captain Owens, I cannot agree with that assessment," King said. "How many times has he been suspended for similar incidents?"

"Three," Owens admitted.

McCarthy, the union rep, interjected, "Officer Maddox's record has no such incidents. His one-year review contains nothing but glowing remarks from his superiors."

"Thank you for that, Mr. McCarthy. Would anyone else like the opportunity to be heard?"

Hearing no responses, King said, "Mr. McCarthy, would you take the two officers to the hall while we make our determination?"

McCarthy, Maddox, and O'Riley rose from their seats and left the hearing room.

Once they had left and the door was closed, Howard King asked grimly, "Are we ready to vote to terminate Officers O'Riley and Maddox?" Everyone nodded. "Okay, all those in favor?"

He, the two other civilians, Chief Allen, and the attorney raised their hands and said, "Aye."

"All those opposed?"

Just the two Police Captains raised their hands and said, Nay."

"The ayes have it. Captain Johnson, will you relieve them of their service weapons and badges?"

"Yes, Mr. King."

Chief Allen said, "We will release the video to the media this afternoon, and the Mayor and I will make a statement afterward."

"Thank you, Chief. This hearing is adjourned," King said.

CHAPTER 9

Dan Burnett

The bed was empty when I awoke—Mia was already up and elsewhere in the house. On my way to the staircase, I found her in a spare bedroom across the hall she had converted into an exercise room. There was a ballet bar along a mirrored wall and an elliptical machine facing the window. She was doing yoga on a mat in the middle of the room with AirPods in her ears. When she saw me passing by, she removed the buds and said, "Good morning, sleepyhead."

"Good morning. I'm happy to see you enjoying yourself this morning."

"I do love yoga. I promised myself to stay as fit as I can for as long as I can."

"Have you had breakfast?"

"Just coffee," she said, stretching her arms above her head and settling into a prayer position.

"Okay, enjoy," I said before heading down the stairs.

After pouring myself coffee, I turned on the news. It was still all about Jerome Jordan and the police. The chief of Police was scheduled to hold a press conference later in the morning. I turned the volume down but left the TV on to monitor the morning's events. The sky had become cloudy, and I could see the wind blowing through the trees—a typical blustery March day. I felt grateful for the few sunny, warm days we had just experienced.

Mia entered the kitchen, still in yoga attire, and poured herself another coffee. She took three strawberries from the big Sub-Zero fridge and joined me at the table.

Noticing the image on the TV, she asked, "Is there anything new about the case this morning?"

"They said the Police Chief will make a statement later this morning. I don't know what time."

"I'll try to hang around for that; remember, I volunteer Thursday afternoons at the Humane Society. What do you have going on today?"

"Nothing. I have to do my timesheet for last week so Jim can do the billing. Other than that, I just want to see what the police Chief has to say. How about I take you to the tapas place downtown for dinner?"

"That sounds delightful; we haven't been there in a while."

I retrieved my laptop, did my timesheet, and returned emails while monitoring the TV. After dressing, Mia was in her office, I assume going through the mail and paying bills. Shortly after 11:00, the cameras focused on the podium at City Hall, and I called out to tell Mia it was coming on. I sat in front of the TV and turned up the volume as she joined me on the couch. A moment later, the mayor and the chief approached the podium in front of a smaller crowd than the previous day.

Chief Allen stepped to the microphones. "Good morning, everyone; thank you for coming. Earlier this morning, the Police Department was served with subpoenas asking for the release of any video images involving Jerome Jordan on March 1. The Attorney General has authorized the release to Attorney Bodner. Because Mr. Bodner called for the release to be made public from this podium yesterday, we will be releasing it to any media in good standing that requests it."

He continued, "You will see images of police conduct that we certainly do not condone. We have opened an internal investigation of the officers involved, and ask that everyone allow us to investigate this matter thoroughly and not engage in any acts of violence. I appreciate your cooperation."

He stepped away from the podium without answering the questions being shouted at him, and both he and the Mayor walked away and entered the building. The network we were watching asked their viewers to stay tuned for the video as soon as it became available, then went to commercial.

Mia sighed, "I'm going to warm up some soup before I go. Would you like a bowl?"

"Sure. Thanks."

I muted the TV but left it on to monitor when the videos appeared. A few minutes later, Mia set two bowls on the table, and I enjoyed it just as much as last night. When we finished, I offered to clean up so she wouldn't be late, and she gave me a quick kiss before heading out the door. I put our bowls in the dishwasher, returned the soup to the refrigerator, cleaned up, and returned to the couch. The station had assembled a team of familiar talking heads to comment on today's events. After turning up the sound, it wasn't long before the videos appeared.

The first was from the patrol car dashcam. The image showed them following Jerome's Honda for a few blocks before they turned on the flashing lights. He pulled over two blocks later, opposite the park. The officers approached the vehicle together on the driver's side and conversed with Jerome through the side window, which was already down. Shortly after that, Officer O'Riley drew his gun, aimed it in the car, and spoke to Jerome in an agitated manner. The two officers continued exchanging words with Jerome.

The image had a strobe light effect due to the flashing patrol car lights. A moment later, Officer Maddox, with his gun in one hand, opened the door with his other, and Jerome stepped out of the car with his hands raised. While standing, Jerome turned to face the vehicle and placed his hands on the roof. Officer Maddox returned his gun to its holster, removed the handcuffs from his belt, put one on Jerome's left hand, pulled his hands behind his back, and hooked up his other hand. I had seen no resistance from Jerome so far.

It was then that Officer O'Riley struck Jerome in the head with his nightstick. He then hit his head on the other side with a two-handed grip. Jerome bent over along the rear passenger window of his car for protection, and Officer Maddox joined in the action using his bare fists, striking Jerome's head and neck. Jerome then collapsed on the ground, and Officer O'Riley began kicking him while Officer Maddox bent over and continued punching him on the back of the head as he lay face down with his hands cuffed behind him. This continued for another minute until they lifted Jerome, dragged his lifeless body to the front tire, and propped him up against it, his head hanging forward. I never saw a Taser being used, as the officer's statements had claimed. Then, Officer Maddox walked toward the patrol car, and it appeared the interior lights went on. I assumed he was calling for backup or an ambulance. I saw Officer O'Riley kick Jerome in the ribs one final time.

A minute later, Officer Maddox returned to stand alongside Jerome's car with his partner while the patrol car lights continued flashing. After another minute, a second patrol car arrived, followed by a truck-body ambulance. The two new cops and three paramedics stood chatting alongside the Honda for a few minutes before two of them kneeled on the ground to check on Jerome.

There did not appear to be any rush to administer aid. More patrol cars and officers arrived before the paramedics unfolded a gurney, strapped Jerome on, and wheeled him out of the picture.

The video ended there, and the news station went to their panel for comments. They were horrified by what they had just seen, and so was I. Even though I'd previously seen the Boonmee camera video, the quality and detail were nothing like this. I expected the bodycam footage to be even more impactful, and I wondered what went through those cops' heads to do what I had just witnessed.

I also wondered if my old partner on the force and best friend, Matt Frost, had seen the video and what he thought about it. I called the 49th Precinct and asked for Detective Frost. After being put on hold momentarily, he came on the line.

"This is Detective Frost."

"Hey, Frosty."

"Hi, Dan. Did you just see the video from White Plains?"

"I did. Am I wrong to be disgusted by it?"

"I am, too. What those cops did was heinous."

"I'm glad you agree. What would cause them to do that? They weren't in any danger—it wasn't built-up adrenaline from a life-threatening confrontation."

"They're just bad seeds, Dan."

"I'll say. How do you think this will play out?"

"I guess they'll be fired and brought up on charges, especially if Attorney Bodner keeps up the media campaign. I've seen the mobs on TV."

"I hope you're right. Keep me posted if you hear more about those guys from inside the department."

"Will do. How have you been?"

As much as I trusted Frosty, I didn't want anyone in the department to know what I had been doing until I knew what I was doing. I answered, "I'm fine; Jim has a new 'in' with the collector car community that keeps us busy."

"Good to hear. Give him my best."

"You got it."

I turned the volume up again and listened to the commentators briefly as they introduced the bodycam footage. We were told only Officer Maddox's bodycam had recorded the encounter. Officer O'Riley was either not wearing his camera, or it had been turned off. The video from Officer Maddox showed the same thing we had seen previously, except up close and personal. Close enough to see Jerome's face be crushed against the pavement with each blow to the head.

There was audio recorded, where we heard the harsh language used by the two cops. The only audible thing we heard from Jerome was, "Take it easy, man!" repeated a few times early on when the beating started. Then, the only sounds were accelerated breathing by Officer Maddox and some grunts and groans that I could not determine the origin of. When the video ended, it was repeated, as I imagined it would be, over and over until something else captured the media's attention.

It was now mid-afternoon, and I called my detective friend Willie Grant at the 50th Precinct, hoping he had seen the videos. He and I worked together in the past, and along with his partner, we solved the murder of Mia's brother a few months ago. I wondered what his take as a Black man would be on O'Riley and Maddox.

"This is Grant," he answered.

"Hi, Willy. It's Dan."

"How've you been, pal?"

"I'm well. And you?"

"Good. I assume you've seen the video from White Plains?"

"Yeah, that's why I'm calling. Have you had any run-ins with those two?" I asked.

"Not personally, but the word is O'Riley is a hothead with a history."

"Have you heard anything specific?"

"Just the usual station house rumors, but I hear he's done this before."

"Let me know if you hear anything else, Willie."

"Don't tell me Bodner has you investigating for him." Willy had the same contact with Seth Bodner as me while working on Mia's brother's murder case.

"Well, he called and asked, but I'm wrestling with siding against other cops."

"I get it, Dan. I'd wrestle with it, too."

"Do you think this attack was racially motivated?"

"I try not to jump to that conclusion, but it sure sounds like it. I've stopped wondering why you never hear about a white kid getting beat up by cops."

"Agreed. Keep my involvement under your hat, would you, Willie?"

"Of course. I have no recollection of this conversation."

"Thanks, buddy. We'll talk soon."

The TV station continued showing loops of all the videos, including the ones from the park surveillance cameras. They all showed the same thing, and I didn't pick up on anything new from the differing angles. I shut off the TV, went upstairs to shower, and prepared for dinner with Mia. After dressing in a pair of creased wool slacks, a soft yellow shirt, and tasseled loafers, I headed downstairs just as Mia entered through the garage.

"You look nice, love, what's the occasion?" she asked.

"I'm just looking forward to a night out with a special lady."

She moved in for a kiss that lingered, setting the tone for the evening. "I'm going to take a bath. Why don't you make us a cocktail? I'll be down in a half hour." She kissed me again before running upstairs.

Encouraged that she shared my vision for the evening, I spent the next few minutes putting some appetizers together. I made a charcuterie board with a few hard and soft cheeses, some crackers, and smoked salmon with capers and baby gherkins. I then shook up a batch of Kettle One martinis, slightly dirty, with blue cheese-stuffed olives. As I was pre-chilling the glasses, she returned to the kitchen wearing a smoky-purple dress that clung to her toned body, with high heels that accented her flawless legs.

I poured our drinks, and when she moved closer to touch glasses, I caught her scent and felt my heart race in anticipation of our evening together. When she noticed the charcuterie board, she said, "Ooh, that looks yummy. Shall we take that to the living room?"

"We shall." I carried the board in one hand, being careful not to spill my martini with the other. She followed with hers, and we sat in our happy place overlooking the water. After we had a few sips of our drinks and had sampled the appetizers, I put my arm around her, and she rested her head on my shoulder. Again, her faint scent was captivating. We sat like this for a while, enjoying the physical contact, when she said, "I hope I'm not ruining the vibe here, but what did the new police videos show?"

"Pretty much the same thing we had seen from the restaurant video, except much clearer. It leaves no doubt that these cops were unprovoked and appeared to revel in the assault. The bodycam footage also had sound; these guys are toast."

"That's just awful," she said as she snuggled again into my shoulder.

We nibbled some more from the board, and when we finished our drinks, I said, "I didn't make a reservation, so maybe if we get there close to 6:00, we won't have to wait to be seated."

"Perfect. The sooner we go, the sooner we can return, and I can get you into bed!"

The name of the restaurant was Barcelona, and the aroma of Spanish spices wafted through the air as we entered. The interior was decorated in deep, warm colors, and even though the lighting was soft, all eyes followed Mia as the hostess seated us along a banquette in the rear. We sat side by side and ordered a pitcher of white sangria, which we had enjoyed before. When the hostess had left, Mia kissed me and said, "This is such a romantic place—I just love it here."

When the waitress delivered the sangria, we ordered a few small plates to share. One was the grilled octopus that we both liked on a previous visit. After discussing the current events around Jerome Jordan, I asked about her day.

She began with a sigh, "Today, the vets put down two large mixed-breed dogs that had been there for ten days—the limit. I spent time with those dogs, and they would have made lovable pets for any family with a big yard."

"I'm not sure I could do that work."

"It's always sad when an animal is put down. When people look for a pet, they always choose the cutest, most purebred dogs, not the ones most in need of a home. It can be tough, but you try not to get attached and focus on the big picture: we still place most of the animals in good homes."

"I admire you for volunteering there, Mia."

After a pause, she changed the subject, "So tell me more about sailing."

I told her about what she could expect on our first day out. She asked all kinds of questions and showed genuine interest in learning. She was excited to meet Hannah and only slightly apprehensive. Mia was a confident woman who had succeeded in most of her life's endeavors.

In her twenties, she established a career in fashion design, working with famous international designers. She married a hugely successful music producer in her thirties and continued her career. In her early forties, when her husband became ill with cancer, she stopped working to care for him. I knew that he died two years later, but I often wondered why she didn't return to her career. Hoping not to stir up sad memories, I asked her to fill me in on that time in her life.

"After Robert died, I was pretty depressed and felt alone. After a month or so of Judy urging me to climb back on the horse, I contacted my friends and associates in fashion. We got together for lunch and a few social events, but it quickly became clear how much fashion had changed while I was away. It's really a business where you need to have your finger on the pulse every day to stay on top, and I felt lost and out of touch."

"You didn't think you could catch up?"

"I probably could have, but I'd be starting all over, looking for a job. Then, when our accountant showed me the financial statement, I realized I didn't need to put myself through all that ever again."

"Do you miss it?"

"Not really. I can spend my time doing whatever I please, and tonight, I'm pleased to be spending it with you, my love," she concluded, hugging my shoulder.

As our small plates arrived, we shared them, commenting on their differing tastes. After a while, sitting the way we were, I began lightly caressing her legs. With no one seated near us, we soon tested the limits of public affection and became anxious to get home. I left some cash on the table, and we headed out.

When we reached her house, we went directly to the bedroom, where she lit candles, dropped her dress on the floor, and confidently stood before me in just high heels and a thong. After the foreplay in the restaurant, the vision before me was too much to handle. I tore off my clothes and pushed her onto the bed. It wasn't long before our animal instincts took over, delivering some initial relief.

After catching our breath, we continued to toy with each other, enjoying our closeness. Within a few minutes, we resumed making love, this time much slower, taking time to individually please each other until we were finally spent. We slept the night soundly, cuddled like spoons.

CHAPTER 10

"Good morning, Dan. I just received the service records for O'Riley and Maddox. Would you like a copy?" Seth asked.

"Yes, I would."

"Okay, I'll send them right over. Let me know what you think."

By the time I refilled my coffee, I saw the confidential email was waiting for me, and sent the files to the printer in Mia's office. Throughout the morning, I read them carefully and determined that while Officer Maddox had a short, unblemished record, Officer O'Riley's record was long and tarnished. He had been disciplined multiple times for aggressive behavior and violence, each time involving someone of color. Looking back at the nearly twenty years he had been on the force, most cops would have advanced in rank to detective or inspector. It was evident the list of disciplinary actions had prevented his advancement.

I recalled a retired psychologist who used to work with police officers who had trouble with stress or needed an evaluation after discharging a firearm.

I knew her from my recovery after being shot in the line of duty five years ago, and I hoped she might be able to help me understand these guys. I did a Google search, found a listing for her, and called.

"Hello," she answered "Is this Anne Gibbs?"

"It is."

"This is Dan Burnett. I was with the NYPD, and you saw me a few years ago after I was injured."

"Yes, I remember you, Dan. How are you?"

"Fully recovered and now retired. I'm working as a P.I. and have come across a case that you might be able to help me with."

"Sure. Tell me about it."

"Can I trust that what I tell you will go no further?"

"Certainly. Since I've seen you professionally, we still have doctor-patient confidentiality."

"Perfect. I am investigating the Jerome Jordan incident and would like a profile of the officers."

"Oh my, a very public case!" she exclaimed.

"I was hoping you could review their service files and determine why they did what they did."

"Sure, can you email them to me?"

"Yes. I'll send them over now."

"Okay. Would you like to come by tomorrow to hear my thoughts?"

We made an appointment for 11:00 the following day before ending the call.

The afternoon had become cloudy and dark, and rain was in the forecast, so my previous plan to spend the day at the marina was out the window. After eating a quick sandwich, I helped Mia in the garden, cleaning and preparing it for the upcoming planting season. Besides flowers, she liked to grow tomatoes and other vegetables. Fortunately, the rain held off just long enough for us to finish.

By morning, it was pouring. Mia and I slept in late, and after shaving and dressing, I joined her in the kitchen and watched her make an omelet while pouring myself coffee. By 10:30, I was on my way to meet Anne Gibbs.

The address she gave me was in a residential neighborhood, and I realized that since she had retired, we were meeting at her home. Standing under an umbrella, I rang the bell at her front door.

When it opened, I said, "Hi, Doc, good to see you."

"Come on in, Dan. Can I take your jacket?"

"Thanks. It's nasty out there this morning."

"It sure is. Would you like anything? Coffee?"

"No thanks," I replied.

"Well, have a seat and make yourself comfortable." She gestured to a sofa in her living room and sat in an adjacent chair. The decor was library-like, with comfortable seating and an overstuffed bookshelf along one wall. I guessed that Anne was a few years older than me with hair that was a natural mixture of blonde and gray. She wore round horn-rimmed glasses that accented her hazel eyes.

"So, how have you been?" I asked.

"Very well, thanks. I'm enjoying retirement."

"Have you formed an opinion on these two cops' motivation?"

"Well, I'm always cautious about expressing an opinion without personally examining the subjects, but there have been many cases over the years involving police brutality, and there are some consistencies among the cases. A common thread is the rush or sense of satisfaction that a pathological bully gets from physically beating another person. It is an experience that can become addictive, like alcohol, opiates, or nicotine. In some ways, it's similar to rape.

After the gratification from that experience, they feel a need to repeat it." She continued, "Judging from his history, I think this was the case with Officer O'Riley. He has been involved in three similar cases since his time with the WPPD, and there were likely more incidents that went unreported for one reason or another. This personality type is more likely to pursue police work than the general population."

"And how about Officer Maddox?"

"He's completely different. I believe he looked up to Officer O'Riley and sought his approval. He was the junior officer and may have considered O'Riley the 'pack leader.' This behavior is well documented not just in humans but also in animals."

"Was there a racist element in play here?"

"Ah, so now we get into a whole other motivation. The numbers show an almost exclusive incidence of police brutality occurring with victims of color. I'm not just speculating here; there is a documented lack of empathy for Black men among many police officers. In reviewing Officer O'Riley's records, every incident of violence involved a person of color. He may indeed be a white supremacist."

"Why do you think we're hearing about more of this recently?"

"Maybe there is just more news coverage of everything these days, but ever since a Black man was elected President, the hatred among white supremacists has grown, and when our last president refused to speak out against it, they felt emboldened. I suspect some felt he was granting them permission. Again, the numbers show that this racist personality type is more likely to pursue police work than the general population."

Anne continued, "There's also a common need among most people to feel like they're better than someone else to boost their standing in society. Of course, a professional analysis would be needed to determine if these theories apply to these individuals."

"Are there any more questions I should be asking?"

"I think we've about covered it, Dan."

"Thanks for this, Doc. Do you do expert courtroom testimony?"

"I have in the past. I'd be willing to do it again for this case."

"Okay. Email me a bill for your time today, and I'll pass it on to the attorney," I said while rising.

We said our goodbyes as I headed out the door, opening my umbrella for the dash to my car. While returning to Mia's, I called Seth and told him about my meeting with Anne and her thoughts. I also told him she would be willing to testify in court if it came to that. He thanked me for the report, and we left it there, promising to keep in touch.

The following day, I went to the hospital to see Jerome with my own eyes. I thought that might help me decide whether or not to continue investigating. When I arrived, his mother and father were there, along with his younger sister. Their despair immediately struck me. Mrs. Jordan was in tears, holding Jerome's hand while her husband tried to comfort her. Their young daughter was leaning over the bed, hugging her brother's legs as if by just maintaining contact, her energy would heal him. I was frozen in the doorway, fighting back my own tears, thinking I should leave them be, when Mr. Jordan noticed me. He stood and introduced himself, expecting me to do the same.

"I'm so sorry to interrupt, Mr. Jordan. My name is Dan Burnett; attorney Bodner has asked me to investigate what happened to your son."

"You're an investigator?"

"Yes, Sir. I've worked with attorney Bodner before. I can see that this is a private time for you and your family. I should leave."

"Let me walk out with you, Mr. Burnett."

As we were on the elevator down, he said, "You know, I had the police talk with Jerome when he got his driver's license. I told him that no matter what reason the police have to pull you over, no matter what insults or mistreatment they dish out, comply with them so you can make it home alive." After a deep breath, he continued, "I thought we had turned the corner as a country a decade ago and put all this behind us. But now, where are we?"

"I don't know—I thought we had turned a corner, too. At least I was hopeful we had."

When the elevator door opened, he said, "Thank you for coming, Mr. Burnett. Please make those cops pay for what they did to my son."

"We will, Mr. Jordan. We're all pulling for Jerome."

With that, I exited the hospital feeling more depressed and con-flicted than ever.

Over the next week, I tried to keep my focus off Jerome Jordan but found myself failing. I tried to stay busy with boat chores and helped Jim with the car collectors. Mia and I still monitored the evening news and knew that while Jerome was still alive, he remained unconscious. The doctors were now speculating that he likely had brain damage and would never fully recover. While the police claimed to be investigating the officer's behavior, Seth kept up the pressure by speaking publicly through the media.

By late March, I was at the marina most days, cleaning and preparing Privateer for the season. Mia came with me a few times to help and asked questions about what this or that did and the purpose of each rope. After explaining that ropes on a boat were referred to as lines and what each one was used for, she seemed to understand and was looking forward to using the knowledge on the water.

The following weekend was warm and sunny, and Hannah offered to come down and help install the sails. I felt this would be as good a time as any to introduce her to Mia. I planned to pick up Hannah on Saturday morning, start working on the boat, and have Mia bring lunch at midday.

When Hannah and I had finished raising the head sail and rolling it up on the furler, we moved on to the mainsail. Fortunately, there was little wind, and we could raise it without drama, sort through the lines, and lower it onto the boom before installing the sail cover. Then I saw Mia walking down the ramp carrying a canvas bag.

"Good afternoon!" she exclaimed.

"Hi, Mia," I replied. After giving her a hand climbing aboard, I made the introductions. They were both smiling as they shook hands and appeared pleased to meet one another, although I sensed a hint of caution from Hannah. I imagined she was initially hesitant to accept another woman filling her mother's role in my life, not knowing if this was temporary or long-term. Regardless, she handled herself with grace.

As I opened the cockpit table, Hannah retrieved placemats, napkins, and utensils from the galley. Once the table was set, Mia took out the items she had purchased at a deli. She had brought roast beef sandwiches, potato salad, cucumber and tomato salad, and a bottle of Rosé. I went below for wine glasses as she handed out the sandwiches and opened the salad containers. We all dug in and enjoyed the meal as Mia asked Hannah about college life and her major.

Hannah was receptive to the questions and appeared comfortable speaking with Mia. She told her about her business finance major and that she wasn't yet sure what kind of job she wanted. The two of them eventually shared laughter, and whatever trepidation I had about this meeting soon disappeared.

After finishing, I went below, and they handed me the remnants of lunch. I put things away and cleaned the dishes, leaving the ladies in the cockpit chatting and enjoying their wine. When there was a pause in their conversation, I returned to the cockpit, where we continued to enjoy the delightful spring day. A while later, Mia excused herself, stating she had some shopping yet to do. She and Hannah said their goodbyes, saying they looked forward to seeing one another again. After Mia left, we locked up the boat and wandered to the car for the drive back to Iona.

Once we were buckled in and on the road, Hannah turned to me and said, "Dad, Mia is beautiful, smart, and classy. You've done well for yourself with her."

"Thank you. I think so, too."

"I suppose in the back of my mind, I was trying to find reasons not to like her, but there were none. I'm happy for you."

"I appreciate that, Han. Are you up for helping me teach her to sail?"

"Sure. I'd like that."

The rest of our conversation was mostly school-related and about her prospects for a job after graduation. She was debating whether she wanted the pressure of Wall Street or to look for something lower-key. I listened but didn't offer advice other than to suggest she find something she enjoys. Big help, Dad.

While driving to Mia's, I looked forward to hearing about her impression of Hannah. As I entered the driveway, Seth called.

"Hi, Dan. I wanted to let you know that Jerome passed today."

"Shit, what happened?" I asked as I shut down the car and slumped in the seat.

"I'm told he stopped breathing in the early morning hours. They put a ventilator on him, but when they did an EEG, they determined there was no brain activity. They found a hemorrhage and internal bleeding on the left side of his brain. It took the family most of the day to let him go. Needless to say, they are devastated."

"So the cops can be charged with murder," I stated.

"If I have anything to say about it, they will. But right now, I'll let the family dictate the pace. They need some time to grieve."

"I would think so. Keep me posted if you can."

"Will do. I will need some investigative work, so I'll need to know if you want in."

"Okay. You'll hear from me soon."

"Thanks, Dan. Goodbye."

I rested my head back, took a deep breath, and let the news of Jerome's death sink in. I guess I was there a while because I saw Mia step out the front door to check on me. As soon as I saw her, I opened my door, pushed Jerome to the back of my mind, and walked toward the house with a smile on my face, knowing she would want to talk about meeting Hannah.

"Well, you certainly impressed Hannah!" I exclaimed. "She said, 'Not only are you beautiful, but smart and classy.' She's happy for us."

"That's great to hear. I was impressed by her, too. And those blue eyes are stunning."

"She's looking forward to sailing with you."

"Really? You raised quite a girl there," she said as she hugged me.

"Would you like a cocktail?" I asked.

"Sure. A Manhattan?"

"Perfect," I said as we closed the front door behind us and strolled to the kitchen with our arms around one another.

After making our drinks and taking our first sip, I said, "I was just speaking to Seth in the car. Jerome Jordan died today."

Her shoulders sank, "Oh, that's so sad. Everyone was pulling for him."

"I know. The cops can now be charged with murder."

"Is that going to affect whether you get involved or not?" she asked.

"It might. The more I think about it, the angrier I get. I keep picturing each blow to his head—that's what killed him."

She nodded and sipped her drink before saying, "I'm sure you'll do the right thing, love."

"Thanks. Do we have dinner plans?"

"I was hoping you would grill some steaks tonight. I bought some nice- looking ribeyes."

"Sounds good," I replied, sitting by the TV and toggling the remote. "Let me know when to start the grill."

I watched the local news as she started prepping for dinner. The story of Jerome's death was just breaking on the networks. They showed some pictures of him in the hospital bed from a few days ago, but I didn't learn anything new. A few minutes after Mia placed potatoes in the oven, she asked me to start the grill. I went outside on the deck, and after lighting it, I leaned on the railing, watching a sailboat on the water. My mind went to the police record of Officer O'Riley and wondered what kind of sick bastard he must be. I was unable to relate at all, but Anne Gibbs's words painted a pretty clear picture.

I retrieved the steaks and placed them on the grill a few minutes later. As they were cooking, the sun was setting over the New York skyline, reminding me how magnificent the views from Mia's house were. Not only was there a view of Long Island Sound, some bridges, and Manhattan, but you could follow the sun from when it rose to when it set. I could not think of anywhere else that offered all that. When the ribeyes were just on the rare side of medium, I carried them inside on a platter, letting them rest for a few minutes while Mia plated the potatoes and a Caesar salad. After I opened a bottle of Cabernet, we sat down to eat.

As delicious as the meal was and as enjoyable as it was to dine with Mia, I could not get Jerome and those cops out of my head. She could tell I was grappling with it and asked what I was thinking.

"I'm sorry, but I never thought I would witness a cop murder someone for personal satisfaction. That goes against every principle I lived by for thirty years. I'm not going to be able to let this go."

She placed her hand on my arm, looked me in the eyes, and said, "You're a good man, Dan Burnett. I knew this was the decision you would come to."

After finishing our meal and cleaning the kitchen, we went upstairs, showered together, and climbed into bed. She kept my mind occupied for the rest of the evening.

CHAPTER 11

The first thing in the morning, I called Seth and told him my decision. He was happy to hear it and asked if I could come in after lunch. We agreed on 1:30. I texted Jim Abbott and asked if he would be in the office today. I said I would see him in an hour when he told me he was already there. After dressing and having a second cup of coffee with Mia, I headed for the office in Scarsdale. While driving, it felt like winter had returned. The sky was dark and cloudy, and I sensed precipitation, either rain or snow, depending on the temperature. Having lived in the area all my life, my bet was on sleet.

When I walked into the office, Jim told me he had heard about Jerome's passing and asked if that had changed my thinking about getting more involved.

"I guess it does. Last week, I witnessed the family grieving at the hospital. Yesterday, when I learned of his death, I found myself filled with anger at those cops, especially O'Riley. I called Seth this morning and told him I was in. We're meeting this afternoon," I said.

"I get it, Dan. You are not wrong for thinking that way. I would probably do the same if I were in your shoes."

I told him about Anne Gibbs' theories on the cops' behavior, and he nodded in agreement while listening.

After catching up on his latest work with the car collectors, we walked a few doors down the street to the Outback Steakhouse, our usual lunch spot. The sky had brightened, and we thought it might remain dry for another hour or so. We each had a Cobb salad, continued our discussion, and then wandered back to our office building, where I left him in the parking lot before driving to White Plains.

When I arrived at Seth's office, Paula buzzed his phone, and he appeared at the door to his inner office, ushering me inside. Once seated in the comfortable cluster, he updated me on the latest events.

"Officers O'Riley and Maddox have been released from the department, and the District Attorney is considering murder charges. I aim to keep up the pressure to see that he does."

"How can I help?" I asked.

"I'd like you to look into O'Riley's background. Find out everything you can about his violent behavior. From your psychologist friend's theories, I think he's the one to make a murder case against. We should know within a few weeks if the DA is serious about bringing charges."

"Okay. I think I should work backward from this case, starting with the previous incident in his report. I'll try to speak with other cops he was partnered with and see what they say. I can go back to when he was in school if I need to," I said.

"Sounds like a plan. Remember that we're looking for witnesses whose testimony will stand up in court."

"Got it, but to begin with, I need to get a feel for this guy, understand his motivation, and see where that leads us," I said.

"Okay. By the way, Jerome's funeral service will be held on Thursday. I'm told some racial and religious leaders are trying to make this a big media event, but that's not what the Jordans want; we'll see how this plays out. Can you make it?"

"For sure. I'll pay my respects to the family, regardless of a media event."

"Great, I'll have Paula forward you the particulars."

After returning to my car, I reviewed O'Riley's police record, focusing on the previous incident of violence more than a year ago; his partner at that time was William Kidd. Since then, Kidd had become a detective and was assigned to homicides. When I called the WPPD and asked for him, I was connected to his voicemail. I hung up, not wanting to make it easy for anyone to know who was snooping around by leaving a name and number. I'd have to figure out a different way to reach him. I searched O'Riley's file to find the next most recent violent incident. That was from two years ago when he was the junior partner with an officer named Kevin Crocker. I called the WPPD again and discovered Officer Crocker had left the department a year ago and was now assigned to the NYPD. I called Matt Frost on his cell, hoping he could locate him for me.

He answered, "Hello, Dan."

"Hey, Frosty. How have you been?"

"I'm okay. I heard about the Jordan kid; that's just terrible."

"Yeah, it is. They're having a service for him this week. Let me know if you want the details."

"Thanks, I will."

"I wanted to see if you could locate a Detective Crocker for me. He transferred from White Plains to NYPD a year or so ago."

"I think I can do that. Do you want to meet for a beer around five?"

"Murph's?"

"Murph's it is," he replied before ending the call.

I had an hour to kill before heading to the Bronx. Trying to think of another way to speak with Detective Kidd, I wandered around the corner, into the police department, and approached the desk sergeant.

"Excuse me, officer. I have some information for one of your detectives but forgot his name. Do you happen to have pictures of them? I might be able to identify him."

With reading glasses perched on the end of his nose, the sergeant reached under his desk and handed me a binder.

"Here's a book with pictures of every officer in the department," he said before returning his attention to whatever he was doing.

I sat on a bench with the book and leafed through it until I saw a headshot of Detective Kidd. He had a puffy face and appeared overweight. After studying the picture for a moment, I continued leafing through the book before returning it to the desk sergeant and said, "I guess my memory is not as good as I thought. I appreciate your help, officer."

I returned to my car and headed down the Bronx River Parkway to meet Frosty at Murph's. When I walked in, I saw his bulldog-like form sitting in a booth, working on a pint of Guinness. Matt Frost is about five-foot-eight and two hundred pounds, all muscle with a thick neck. While five years younger than me, he had gray hair and wore it cut short. Murph's was a typical cop bar and had remained unchanged for all the years I went there. The interior was dark wood, the booths were worn, and old neon beer signs hung on the walls. One sign was for Rheingold Beer, which hadn't been made in decades.

I sat in the booth across from Frosty, and Murph appeared with a cold bottle of Heineken for me. He set it down and walked away with just a nod. Matt and I touched our beers, and he said, "Kevin Crocker is a homicide detective with Manhattan North, out of the 24th precinct. He has a good rep."

"Thanks for that. He used to partner with one of the cops who killed Jerome."

"So you've decided to work with Bodner?"

"Yeah, I have. After watching the video over and over and learning more about O'Riley, I can't let it go."

"You need to be careful here, Dan. There is no way to know how far he and his buddies will go to protect him."

"I'll be careful. I don't plan to confront him; I'm just gathering information to help Seth make a case."

"They'll still try to stop you."

"I know. I'll keep a low profile, but I need to speak to his former partners."

He studied my face for a moment, making sure I understood the gravity of the situation. Then he said, "So, how is Hannah doing?"

"She's fine. Last week, she came to the boat and helped me put the sails on. She also met Mia."

"How did that go?"

"All good. She says she wants to help Mia learn how to sail."

"Good to hear—that could have gone another way."

"For sure. Hannah says she's happy for me."

"You know, the sun always seems to shine favorably on you, Dan." I shrugged my shoulders at his observation.

When I arrived at Mia's that evening, I found her at her desk, went around behind her, and began to massage her neck. I told her about the service for Jerome on Thursday.

"I'd like to go too if you don't mind some company," she said.

"I would love your company," I said, kissing the top of her head.

CHAPTER 12

Sean O'Riley

Detective Kidd and Sean O'Riley were eating bacon and eggs at a coffee shop on the south side of town, discussing the news that Jerome Jordan had died. Kidd said, "The D.A. is going to bring murder charges, Sean. The public will demand it."

"What should I do?"

"You just have to ride it out and let the union attorneys deal with it."

"I can't just sit by and wait for my life to come apart. There has to be something I can do."

"We need to find out where Bodner is getting his information. He was awfully quick to get those eyewitness statements."

"And the restaurant video. He must have an investigator working for him, someone who went out and canvassed the neighborhood," O'Riley said.

"We need to find out who that is."

"Are you thinking of taking him out?" O'Riley asked.

"Christ, we're not talking about murder here. We can just follow him and see what he's up to; maybe scare him off."

"I'm up for it: I've nothing else to do now."

"You shouldn't be out there pretending to be a cop; I can join you this afternoon, and we'll go together."

"Thanks. I'll meet you in Tibbets Park at 1:00."

After paying their bills, they exited the coffee shop, and Detective Kidd went to work while Sean O'Riley spent the morning among the unemployed.

That afternoon, the two of them began canvassing the area where the beating occurred. They saw the reward posting on the bulletin board at an apartment building and asked the super about it. He told them someone had come in a week ago and thumbtacked it on the board but knew nothing more about it. O'Riley removed and pocketed the notice.

At the next building, the door was locked, so they rang the super. When he opened the door, Detective Kidd flashed his badge and asked if anyone had posted a reward notice. The super led them to the bulletin board near the mailboxes and showed them the notice. After removing it, he asked if any residents had followed up on the reward.

"I think the lady in 307 might have spoken to him, but I'm not sure. You're welcome to go ask her."

"Thank you; we'll do that."

Kidd and O'Riley rode the old elevator to the third floor and knocked on the door to 307. After a moment, the door opened a few inches—the limit of the chain. "Yes, may I help you?"

After Kidd flashed his badge, he said, "Hello, Ma'am. Did you speak with anyone about the traffic stop across the street last week?"

"No, I don't know anything about that," she replied.

"Are you sure? We heard that you spoke to someone about it."

"Nope. Not me."

"Okay, sorry to bother you, ma'am."

On the way down in the elevator, O'Riley said, "That welfare queen is lying; I can just tell."

Kidd nodded knowingly, and they left the building. Having exhausted the neighboring residences, they tried to figure out where the door camera video might have come from. Recalling that it was shot from across the park over low- growing foliage, they spotted the Boonmee Thai restaurant. After crossing the street, they entered and spoke to the owner after flashing a badge.

Kidd asked, "Did you supply security footage of the traffic stop to anyone a week or so ago?"

"Yes. Or I should say the security company did. They sent the video to a man who came in from an attorney's office."

"Do you know his name?"

"I don't remember, but the security company might still have it. Here's their number," he said, handing them a business card.

"Thank you. You've been a big help."

Kidd and O'Riley wandered across the street to the park. Kidd used his cell phone to make the call and identified himself as the police. After holding for a minute, he had a name, Dan Burnett, and an email address.

With that information, it was easy enough for him to obtain Dan Burnett's address, license plate, and car info from the DMV once back at the station. With a little more research, he discovered that he was a former NYPD detective and called O'Riley to share the information.

"He's a former cop?" O'Riley exclaimed. "And he's investigating other cops? Fuck him!"

"Do you want to check out his address?"

"For sure. I'll do that right now."

"All right. Let me know what you find out."

O'Riley hopped in his Mustang and made the half-hour drive to City Island. He recalled being there before, and once he crossed the bridge, he was reminded there was just one road with a turn-around at the far end. He discovered the address was a marina and, after poking around a bit more, concluded that Burnett must live on a boat. Who the fuck lives on a boat?

The next morning, O'Riley arrived in front of attorney Bodner's office building and found a parking spot with a good view of the parking garage entrance. He watched all the people walking by, imagining their jobs and trying to come up with a story in his mind for each of them, something he often did to pass the time. It wasn't long before he realized how many of them were non-white, and his rage began to build. The Blacks and Asians were taking all the good jobs away from white Americans, he thought. Some of them were well-dressed and walked the street like they belonged, and he feared that pretty soon, he would be a minority in his own country. When he saw a Black man walking hand in hand with a blonde woman, the desire to attack them became overwhelming. He did some deep breathing exercises he learned in an anger management class— a class he was forced to take the last time he was suspended.

It was the middle of the afternoon when he saw the Grand Cherokee enter the parking garage. After a few minutes, he took a tracking device from the glove compartment and wandered into the garage. Every space was filled on the lower floors, and he started climbing the ramps from floor to floor, looking for Burnett's car. Nearly exhausted, he spotted it on level five. After confirming the license number, he placed the magnetic tracker under a wheel well and took the elevator down.

Later that evening, Sean O'Riley called William Kidd. "I put a tracking device on Burnett's car and texted you a link. Can you take over tomorrow so we have a new tail vehicle?"

"Sure. If we can follow him to a family member, get a picture, and send it to him, he might realize that he's jeopardizing their safety."

"Do we even know if he has a family?"

"A guy his age must have a wife or kids. Hopefully, he'll lead us to them."

"Can you do a DMV search for a prior address?"

"Yeah, I'll do that, too. I'll call you in the morning with what I find out."

"Talk to you then," O'Riley said before hanging up.

CHAPTER 13

Dan Burnett

Contemplating how to speak with Detective Kidd and Detective Crocker, I thought it best just to call their precincts and ask for them. First, I tried Kidd at WPPD.

"Hello, may I speak with Detective Kidd?"

"Hold, please."

A minute later, I heard, "This is Kidd."

"Hello, I have been hired by Jerome Jordan's family to inquire about the officers involved."

"And your name is?" he asked.

"I work for Attorney Seth Bodner; any inquiries about the investigation should be directed to him."

"No comment." He hung up.

I paused to reflect on how that call went and devised a different tactic before calling Detective Crocker at the 24th precinct.

"Detective Crocker, please."

"Just a moment."

"Crocker speaking."

"Hello, I'm calling from Attorney Seth Bodner's office about the incident involving Jerome Jordan."

"How can I help you?"

"I understand you worked with Officer O'Riley in White Plains."

"I did, but that was a few years ago," he said.

"I also understand you were involved in a police brutality incident with him. I was hoping to get your impressions of Officer O'Riley."

"He was a nut job. I asked for a new partner immediately after that incident, and I'm not surprised to hear he was involved in the Jordan attack."

"How was he a 'nut job'?"

"Look, I don't know you, and I should not speak ill of fellow officers," he said.

"Would you be willing to speak with me if I met you privately, off the record?"

"Maybe. I'm off at 2:00 today. I could meet you at the 97th Street entrance to Central Park. That's if I don't change my mind."

"I'll be there, Detective Crocker. Thank you," I said before ending the call.

I was happy that the telephone tactic worked better, but perhaps it was just because he was more removed from O'Riley than Detective Kidd. And it would still be useless if he didn't show up.

After lunch, I drove into Manhattan. Sitting on a park bench just inside the park entrance, I noticed some buds on the trees and some squirrels on the move, confirming that spring was on its way.

I scouted each face that entered the park, hoping to identify the detective.

Eventually, a tall man wearing a well-worn tie and sport coat entered the park. From the holster bulge under his arm, I assumed it was Crocker. He looked at me, we made eye contact, and I nodded before he sat on the bench next to me.

"Detective Crocker?" I said.

"That's right. I only have a few minutes," he replied.

"Thank you for coming. I'm trying to find out as much as I can about Sean O'Riley. I'm sure you heard that Jerome Jordan died a few days ago, and the doctors say it was from blows to his head. O'Riley's record shows this wasn't the first time he beat someone while in uniform."

"I only witnessed it once but heard it had happened a few other times."

"Tell me about the time you witnessed."

"It went down pretty much like what I heard about the Jordan attack. We were in the patrol car, and he was determined to pull someone over. When we witnessed a Black guy who didn't come to a complete stop before making a right turn, O'Riley lit the lights and pulled him over. He seemed agitated and looking for trouble."

"What happened next?"

"It should have been just a license and registration verification, but when he ordered the guy out of the car, I approached them to assist my partner, assuming something was irregular. O'Riley ordered the guy to put his hands on the roof with his legs apart and began a rough search. Then, out of the blue, he started clubbing the guy on the head. After a few blows, I grabbed O'Riley, pulled him away, and got between them. Being the senior officer, I ordered him back to the patrol car to call it in and request backup. I had never seen a fellow cop go off like that. We let the guy go with a warning, but his lawyer pressed charges two days later. There was an investigation, and we were both reprimanded because I was the senior officer. I heard the city settled the case monetarily, but my opportunities for advancement were over. A few months later, I was able to get transferred to the NYPD, took some classes, and am now a detective, 2nd grade."

"Would you be willing to testify to that on the record?"

"Not voluntarily. But If subpoenaed, that's the story I would tell because it's the truth."

"Thank you, Detective. As a former cop, I understand the pressure you're under to support your fellow officers and the department."

"Are we done here?" he asked.

"Yes, we are." I handed him my card and said, "Thank you again."

I remained seated as he left the park the same way he came. A clearer picture of Sean O'Riley was forming in my mind, confirming that he had to be kept off the streets. I called Seth and relayed my discussion with Detective Crocker, including what he had told me about testifying. Seth asked if he would be credible on the witness stand, and I replied, "Absolutely."

"That's good to hear. While I've got you, I need to let you know that Paula has fielded some phone inquiries about how we discovered the Boonmee video and who found the eyewitnesses. Of course, she did not release your name, and the callers would not state theirs when she asked if they wanted a callback from me. My guess is that it was the police fishing for information."

"Thanks for the heads-up. Have you heard if the District Attorney will be charging Officers O'Riley and Maddox?"

"I haven't heard a thing. They'll probably drag their feet on the investigation to gauge public opinion. In the meantime, I'll do everything I can to keep the public engaged."

"Okay. I'll keep plugging away."

"Be careful out there. I'd like to keep your identity unknown for now."

"Will do, Seth. I agree," I said before ending the call.

While walking to my car, I wondered if my call to Detective Kidd prompted the inquiries about my efforts. When I reached the car, I received a phone call from Mr. Boonmee, who informed me the police had been in, asking about the door camera video. He said, "They specifically asked who I gave it to, and I told them about the security company, and they told them your name. I immediately realized my mistake, so I wanted to let you know."

"I understand. I appreciate the call."

"I'm sorry, Mr. Burnett."

"Don't worry about it," I replied before ending the call.

Well, keeping my name out of it didn't last long.

While driving to Mamaroneck, I called Mia with my ETA, and she informed me that she was making homemade linguini with white clam sauce. I picked up a bottle of Pinot Grigio on the way. Like everything Mia makes, It was delicious.

The next day was Thursday. Paula had emailed me the schedule for the funeral service. It would be held at 10:00 at a small local church where the Jordan family were parishioners, followed by the burial at Mount Cavalry Cemetery. She offered to get to the church early to save seats for us.

When we arrived, we saw the media set up outside the church on the sidewalk, with politicians and racial leaders fighting for a moment in front of the cameras. There was the same crowd of people holding signs that were at the previous news conferences. We walked past the melee and into the packed church, where people were standing behind the last row. With an organ playing a somber tune, I spotted Seth and Paula along the aisle directly behind Jerome's family. They slid over to make room for us, and once seated, I quietly introduced them to Mia. Jerome's father recognized me, turned to shake my hand, and thanked me for coming. While waiting for the service to begin, I admired the beautiful stained glass window at the front depicting Jesus holding out his hands to welcome us.

The minister opened the service with a prayer: "Eternal rest, grant unto them, O Lord, and let perpetual light shine upon them. Through the mercy of God, rest in peace."

Jerome's mother began to cry, and we could see her shoulders trembling.

Her daughter hugged her arm while her husband held her hand. Seeing her grieve caused Mia and I to tear up, and she clung to my arm.

The minister started his sermon by addressing the Jordan family directly. It was apparent he knew Jerome well, and he spoke about his goals in life, his college studies in biology, and his vision for his future. He spoke at length about Jerome's accomplishments in school sports and his commitment to the church. He raised the question of how God could allow someone with seemingly their whole life ahead of them to die so tragically, then went on to say that God never promised we wouldn't die. In fact, he promised the opposite—everyone dies on this earth and then lives forever in heaven. He told us that God is all-knowing and has another plan for Jerome. Mrs. Jordan continued sobbing as many others in the congregation held tissues to their eyes as the sermon continued.

After we sang a few hymns, he quoted some scripture and concluded with a memorable phrase: "The Lord is close to the broken-hearted; he rescues those whose spirits are crushed."

As the organ resumed playing, the minister guided the Jordan family to the rear of the church, where he stood with them in a receiving line. We were among the last to share words with them, and once outside, we saw the crowd still there, waiting for the family to exit. Seth, who everyone knew from his time on television, stood on the top step and asked everyone to respect the family's privacy wishes on this solemn day.

When the Jordans exited the church, the cameras were rolling, but everyone silently showed them respect, clearing a path for them to walk to the limousine parked at the curb.

The procession of cars following them to the cemetery was the longest I had ever seen. The police blocked traffic along the way, and when we arrived, the TV news trucks and many people who could not fit in the church were already there.

Regardless of the large crowd, the minister led a simple burial service. He recited a few more prayers, and then the family tossed the first shovels of dirt on the casket. Mrs. Jordan seemed to have partially regained her composure, or perhaps she had no more tears left to shed. Mia and I silently slipped away while their close friends remained to comfort them. On our way out, we saw the politicians and racial leaders still speaking in front of the cameras.

CHAPTER 14

Over my morning coffee, I reviewed O'Riley's record, looking for where to go next. It was apparent that any additional effort to speak with Detective Kidd would be fruitless, so I focused on his previous partners. I turned off the location services on my phone, which I'd have to turn back on to use the navigation app.

Even though my name was already known, I didn't want to make it easy for them to track me from my cell phone number. Sure, they would have to get a judge to issue a warrant, but I knew all the tricks they could use. Once again, I called the White Plains police station. This time, I asked for Officer Sanchez. I ended the call when I was told he wasn't expected until noon. I planned to stop by the station then and try speaking with him in person.

Mia joined me at the kitchen table in her yoga attire and, after her first sip of coffee, asked what my plans were for the day.

"I'm going up to White Plains around lunchtime to try to speak with one of O'Riley's former partners. I thought I would stop by the marina this morning. Would you like to come?"

"I was planning on exercising this morning. How about tomorrow?"

"Sure. The weather looks great this weekend. Maybe I'll see if Hannah would like to go for a sail with us?"

"That sounds wonderful."

"Okay, it's too early to call her now, but I'll let you know later."

"Perfect!" she said before heading upstairs with her coffee.

The seagulls were enjoying the morning at the marina. Dozens of them flew about as I strolled down the ramp, their calls welcoming me. Once aboard Privateer, I set about getting her ready for the weekend. Now that there were no worries about water freezing, I filled the water tanks from a hose on the dock and started the engine to check that the cooling water was flowing from the exhaust. I let the engine warm up to ensure the thermostat was functioning properly and the alternator was charging. I turned the refrigerator on and everything else electrical, including the navigation and anchor lights. The port- side navigation bulb needed replacing, but I deemed her ready to go once that was done. After shutting everything down and rinsing her off with the hose, I headed up the Hutchinson River Parkway to White Plains.

When I walked into the police station, I asked to see Officer Sanchez and was told to have a seat. A few minutes later, a smallish Hispanic man, no older than thirty, appeared at a doorway and motioned me into a conference room.

I introduced myself as an investigator with Attorney Bodner's office and saw a look of hesitancy cross his face. So far, he had not said a word.

When I told him I was there to discuss Officer O'Riley, his eyes widened, and he put his finger to his lips, indicating not to say anything more. I assumed the conference room was being recorded, and he wanted to remain silent. He tore a page from his pocket note-pad and scribbled a phone number, with instructions to call him this evening. He then opened the door and walked me out. Once outside, I realized I had never heard his voice.

With nothing left to do for the day, I wandered over to Tibbets Park and sat on a bench to call Hannah while soaking in some sun.

"Hi, Dad."

"Hey, Han. I'm calling to see if you'd like to go for a sail tomorrow and Introduce Mia to sailing."

"Sounds good. The weather looks perfect with wind out of the northeast at fifteen knots."

"Happy to hear it. What time should we pick you up?"

"Any time after 9:00 works for me."

"Okay, let's say 9:30. We'll bring lunch."

"I'll be ready and waiting. Bye, Dad."

I guess I had made a sailor out of Hannah after all. Who else would follow wind forecasts?

I continued walking across the street to the apartments where I had left the reward notices, just to make sure they were still there. At the building where Rose Cooper lives, I followed another resident through the door to the bulletin board near the mailboxes. I saw the reward notice was no longer there. On my way out, the super approached and told me that the police had been in asking questions and took the notice down. I rang the super at the next building and asked if he would speak with me. He buzzed the door open a moment later and met me in the lobby. I asked if the notice was still posted, and just like at the last building, he told me the police had been in and took it with them. I thanked him for his time and wandered back to my car. Along the way, I called Rose Cooper and asked if the police had questioned her.

"They were here, but I told them I knew nothing about it. Attorney Bodner didn't give them my name, did he?"

"No, I'm sure he did not. The police were just fishing; you did the right thing."

"That's good to hear. Bye, Dan."

After I reached the car and pulled out into traffic, I noticed a black Ford Explorer behind me. On the ramp to Route 287, I saw it was still there, with a few cars between us. *It's nothing to be concerned about—anyone heading south from White Plains would take the same route,* I thought.

Twenty minutes later, it was still behind me after I had taken the exit for I95. My gut told me I was being followed, so I exited at the first opportunity and stopped at a gas station on US1. The Explorer continued past as I filled the tank. Shortly after that, I got on the westbound ramp toward Mamaroneck and could again see the Explorer a half dozen cars behind me. I now knew I was being followed, and not very skillfully, but he had stayed too far away for me to get a plate number. I wasn't going to let them follow me to Mia's, so I continued west into Pelham and then to the marina on City Island. I rechecked the mirror as I crossed the bridge and no longer saw the Explorer. I assumed they knew where I was heading.

After boarding the boat and opening a Heineken, I called Mia to tell her I was spending the night aboard. Not wanting to worry her about being followed, I made an excuse that I had things to prepare for our sail tomorrow. When I told her I was picking Hannah up at 9:30, she offered to drive herself in the morning and pick up lunch along the way. We chatted for a few more minutes before saying good night.

The day must have rattled me more than I thought because I almost forgot to call Officer Sanchez. When I dialed the number he gave me, he answered in a soft voice with just a mild accent.

"Thank you for speaking with me, Officer Sanchez. As I mentioned before, I'm working with Attorney Bodner regarding the death of Jerome Jordan. I would like to know what you can tell me about Officer O'Riley."

After a brief pause, he said, "I hate him. When we were partnered, he would call me a spic or a wetback every single day. I was born and raised here, and I've served my country. I am a proud American—he's just a racist pig."

"What can you tell me about the incident in which he was suspended for two years ago?"

"He had a chip on his shoulder and always seemed to be looking for a fight. One evening, we were on patrol on Old Mamaroneck Road near Hartsdale Avenue. A couple of young Black guys were driving the other way with a headlight out. As he turned the car around to follow them, I could sense his excitement building. When we pulled them over, he approached the driver's side and demanded the driver get out of the car. When I saw that, I got out of the patrol car, assuming he had a reason for ordering him out. He then told me to frisk him, which I did, but I found nothing. O'Riley accused them of being gang bangers and wanted to know what gang they belonged to. When the guy told him he wasn't in a gang, O'Riley called him a liar and whacked him on the head with his nightstick."

"And you saw no reason for O'Riley to escalate the stop?"

"None. The guy fell to his knees and covered his head with his arms as O'Riley kept beating him. He then kicked him in the ribs, left him on the road, and returned to the patrol car. I followed, and as we drove off, he wiped the sweat off his face and head with a towel he kept on the seat. I'll never forget that image."

"Did you remain his partner?"

"That was the last time. I reported the incident to our watch commander, and he must have reviewed the patrol car video because O'Riley was suspended the next day."

"Is there anything else you can tell me about him?"

"No, except I heard that wasn't the only time he went off like that."

"Thank you, Officer Sanchez. Will you testify to that in a deposition?"

"If I'm under oath, I will tell the truth."

After ending the call, I wrote some notes about the conversation for my report to Seth; then, my mind went back to being followed today.

While working on my second beer, I called Jim Abbott and told him about being followed.

"You've struck a nerve with someone at the WPPD. I would be concerned."

"I am. That's why I'm staying on the boat tonight instead of at Mia's."

"How secure are you on the boat?"

"Well, you need a keycard to enter the gates that lead to the docks."

"Are there guards or a night watchman?"

"Not at this time of the year. It's pretty well lit, though, and there's video surveillance."

"At least there's something." He paused. "If they know who you are, would they know about Hannah or your ex-wife?"

After a long exhale, I said, "Shit. I haven't even considered that."

"You might think about backing off entirely. There is no point in putting your family at risk for some guys who are going to jail anyway."

"You sound pretty confident of that outcome."

"From what I have seen on TV, it sounds like a slam-dunk murder case."

"I hope you're right. I'm going sailing for the weekend with Hannah and

Mia. Let's talk again on Monday."

"For sure. Be careful, Dan."

"I will. Thanks."

Later that night, I slept fitfully aboard Privateer, keenly aware of every motion or sound with my Glock beside me.

Hannah was waiting outside her dorm as promised the following day. She ran to the car carrying her foulie jacket and a backpack. From experience, she knew it could be cold on the water this early in the season.

While chatting with her in the car, I watched the rearview mirror for any signs of a tail and saw none. When we arrived at the marina, Mia was sitting inside her Mercedes SUV in the parking lot, and I made a mental note to get her a keycard. After Hannah and I exited my car, I was pleased to see Hannah rush over to greet Mia with a warm hug. The three of us walked down the ramp, remarking on the beautiful day as Mia expressed her excitement about finally sailing on Privateer.

While I stowed our stuff below, Hannah took Mia around the deck and explained everything that needed to be done before leaving the dock. Once I had warmed the engine, they cast off the lines, and we were underway. Hannah showed Mia where to stow the fenders before taking seats in the cockpit. The temperature dropped dramatically after getting away from the land, and we all put our jackets on. Once out of the channel, I headed into the wind while Mia helped Hannah raise the sails. When I headed off onto a beam reach, Hannah trimmed the sails as Mia watched intently. I shut off the engine, engaged the autopilot, and sat next to Mia, enjoying the silence, the lapping of the waves, and the glory of it all.

A minute later, with a smile on her face, Mia said, "So this is what sailing is all about? I can see why people get hooked on it."

Hannah and I just nodded. If the wind stayed the same, we would be anchored in Hempstead Harbor for lunch in a couple of hours. It wasn't long before Hannah got bored just sitting there. She took the helm, clicked off the autopilot, and tested her hand at steering for the first time this year. Within minutes, she was anticipating the waves and wind gusts and held a steady course. Mia was paying close attention while I pointed out the nuances of what Hannah was doing.

Later, after dropping the mainsail and entering the harbor, we found a spot sheltered from the wind to anchor. Hannah headed Privateer into the wind while I rolled up the headsail. When we had coasted to a stop, I dropped the anchor off the bow, waited for us to drift backward, and then tied off the anchor line.

Within seconds, the anchor grabbed, and we pointed directly into the current.

Voila!

In the shelter of the harbor, it was warm enough to take our jackets off. A few other boats were anchored within sight—much fewer than there would be mid-summer. I went below, passed up three Heinekens, and we celebrated our first sail of the year. Mia was smiling, I thought, not only because of the sail but also because Hannah had accepted her and was enjoying her company. A while later, I passed up the lunch that Mia had brought. It was Middle Eastern food: falafel, hummus, pita bread, and some broccoli salad with raisins and sunflower seeds. I knew she had Hannah in mind when purchasing it, and Hannah loved all of it.

On the way back across the sound, Mia took the wheel while Hannah stood alongside her, coaching her on what to do. I was proud of Hannah for sharing the knowledge I had taught her many years ago.

When we had returned to the marina and were tied up in the slip, we sat around the cockpit, relaxing as the sun dipped lower in the sky. Hannah told us she wanted to return to the dorm before dinner, which she planned to have with her boyfriend, Ken. I had promised Mia that I would take her to Sammy's, one of the many seafood places on City Island, for a crab dinner, so she hung out on the boat while I drove Hannah back to Iona. While Hannah and Mia hugged goodbye on the dock, I looked around the parking lot for anything nefarious before heading up the ramp. Once on the road, I again kept an eye on the mirror and saw no indication of anyone following. We chatted along the way, with Hannah telling me how much she enjoyed her time with Mia. Maybe Frosty was right—the sun does shine favorably upon me.

When I returned to Privateer, Mia had changed into a snug-fitting knit dress in preparation for dinner out. She also had made a shaker of Manhattans for us to enjoy before dinner. We sat below in the warmth of the salon, sipping our drinks. When I suggested we spend the night on the boat, she agreed enthusiastically, and we made up the forward berth before strolling to Sammy's. I had also laid out some towels and turned on the heat and hot water so it would be cozy upon our return.

Rocco, the maître d' at Sammy's, found us a semi-quiet table overlooking the water, and we started with a bottle of Chardonnay while perusing the menu. The last time we were here, we shared the crab platter, and although we loved it, we were a mess and covered in butter by the time we had finished. This time, we ordered Crabmeat au gratin, which we could eat with a knife and fork like civilized people. After finishing our meal, we skipped dessert and returned to Privateer with amorous thoughts on our minds. Once aboard, we slipped off our clothes and climbed into the V-berth. Unlike Mia's giant bed, we were wedged into the bow of the boat. Not that it mattered; we would be all over each other for the next half-hour or so, regardless of the confines.

CHAPTER 15

Sunday was a lazy day. We lounged around the boat, drinking coffee, then wandered up to the diner next to the marina parking lot for a late breakfast. After that, I followed Mia to her house, staying well behind and on the lookout for anyone following us.

Well rested from the weekend, I rose early on Monday, emailed Seth the details of my conversation with Officer Sanchez, and told him about being followed on Friday. I thought more about my conversation with Jim and became concerned about Hannah's safety. After Mia and I had breakfast, I drove to Iona to get a measure of the campus security. I knew a keycard was needed to access her dorm, but as I wandered around the spread-out campus, I realized anyone could just walk into the classrooms, the gym, or the cafeteria. At the administration building, I asked for the head of security and was told to have a seat while they located him. A few minutes later, a forty-ish, well-fed bald man approached me and introduced himself as Ron Horton. He was wearing a sweater with suede elbow patches. We shook hands, and he led me to his office, which wasn't much more than a closet with no windows. A bank of video screens on one wall showed the feeds from a dozen security cameras.

I told him who I was, my history with the NYPD, and my concern for my daughter. He was candid about the vulnerabilities on campus and asked if Hannah knew to be on the lookout. I told him I planned to speak to her today about it. He offered to keep a guard posted in her dorm at night for the next week or until I told him the threat was over. After thanking him, I found my way out and called Hannah.

"Hi, Dad. What's up?"

"I'm in the neighborhood and wanted to see if we could have lunch."

"Sure. My next class is at 1:00."

"How about we meet at noon at the diner near your dorm?"

"Great, see you then."

While strolling through the campus, I stopped to watch how people came and went to the dorms. Most people swiped their keycard on the way in, but if someone was coming out, they usually held the door for someone coming in. Assuming they knew the person, that was no big deal, but I wondered if a student would extend that courtesy to a stranger.

When I walked into the diner, Hannah was waiting for me. After a quick hug, we were seated across from one another in a booth away from the door. The building was an expanded version of a New England-style diner, similar to the one near the marina. It had a brick exterior, with an added dining room on the right side. The rest of the interior was a typical diner, with booths along the front windows, a lunch counter at the rear, and the kitchen beyond that. The lighting was bright, and plates and silverware were clanging. After ordering chicken salad sandwiches, Hannah asked what I was doing in the neighborhood.

"Well, Han, I believe you know I've been investigating the police beating of Jerome Jordan?"

She nodded.

"Last week, I interviewed a few of Officer O'Riley's former partners, and someone was following my car on Friday." I paused to gauge her reaction.

"Do you think it was someone with the police department?" she asked. "I'm not sure, but if it wasn't a White Plains cop, it was Officer O'Riley himself or a friend of his. I'm sure they're just trying to scare me off. But I'm concerned for your safety, Han. I just spoke with Mr. Horton, the head of campus security. He will put a guard in your dorm at night for the time being."

"Oh my god, Dad. This is creepy. Should I stay home with Mom?"

"Would you feel safer there?"

"I don't know. I never thought I should be afraid of the police!"

When the waitress delivered our sandwiches, Hannah just stared at hers. "Regardless of where you stay, I want you to be on guard for anything unusual," I said.

"Could Mom be in danger, too?"

"I doubt it. If someone was trying to scare me off, they might try to scare you, too."

"Let me think about this for the rest of the day."

"That's fine. I'll call your Mom and give her a heads-up as soon as we're done here."

"Okay, I'll talk with her before making a decision."

She finally picked up her sandwich and began eating. I followed her lead, and we remained silent until we finished. After I paid at the counter, we stepped outside, where she hugged me before heading off to class. I sat on a bench along the sidewalk and called her mother, my ex-wife, Sheila.

"Hello, Dan. I haven't heard from you in a while."

"I know, I'm sorry about that." I went on to tell her everything I had just told Hannah.

"Do you mean to tell me that after worrying about you for decades with the police department, I now have to worry about our daughter with your new detective thing?" The vitriol in her voice was readily apparent.

"Again, I'm sorry, Sheila. Hannah and I discussed if she wanted to stay with you instead of at her dorm. She's going to talk to you about it. Please call me after you speak with her."

"I will," she said before hanging up abruptly.

The main reason for our divorce was her fear that I would not come home from work at the end of the day. After recovering from a gunshot wound a few years ago, my return to police work was mainly behind a desk, shuffling papers and answering the phone. She was happy about that, but I hated it. When I returned to active duty, it was too much for her. I moved onto the boat, and she took a job as a middle school librarian, which was her career before we had Hannah.

She enjoys the work, has the summers off, and will get a teacher's retirement. Sheila is fifty-four, one year younger than me, takes care of herself, and has maintained the same brown hair color she had when we met.

With the rest of my day open, I headed back to the marina. While driving, Seth called. "Thanks for the report on Officer Sanchez, Dan. I'm sorry it took so long to reply; I was in court all morning. Tell me more about being followed."

I filled in all the details of my earlier message and told him of my discussion with Jim about being afraid for my loved ones and that I was considering backing off again for the time being.

"I agree that you should back off. There's no point in us going out on a limb if the DA brings charges. It will then be up to him to do the investigation. You've discovered enough already for me to keep the media focused. Listen, we can cover the cost if you think we need to hire private security for you or your family. The money from the GoFundMe page has been pouring in since Jerome died."

"Thanks for that, Seth. I'll let you know about the security."

"Okay. We'll talk soon."

Now that I had backed off, I felt guilty for not telling Mia about being followed. I got off the next exit, turned around, and returned to Mamaroneck with my eyes on the mirror. When I arrived at her house, I found Mia tending her garden in the backyard. She was kneeling, wearing gloves and a hat, and using a small hand shovel. I carried two glasses of iced tea down the deck stairs and sat on the grass alongside her.

"Hi, love. What brings you home so early today?"

"Well, I just got off the phone with Seth. We've concluded I should stop investigating the case for now."

"What brought this about?" she asked, pausing her work to look at me. "I think I was being followed on Friday. I didn't tell you because

I didn't want to worry you. But after speaking with Jim and Seth, I thought it best that you know."

"You kept that from me all weekend?" she asked while resuming her digging.

Sensing she was upset with me, I said, "I didn't want anything to spoil our weekend, Mia. I had been looking forward to it so much." Until now, we have never had a disagreement, and I had no experience measuring her anger. She remained quiet and kept working. "Are you mad at me?" I asked.

Still focusing on her work, she said, "I'm not sure. Let's see how I feel about it in a while." Now, she paused to look at me and took a sip of her iced tea, sitting on her heels.

"I discussed this with Hannah and her Mother today. I felt it was important to warn everyone to be aware and cautious."

"Does that include me?"

"Of course. That's why I didn't come here Friday afternoon when I was being followed."

"But you told me you had things to prepare on Privateer."

"I did have things to do. I just didn't tell you the rest of it."

"I see," she said, now with her head down, focused on her work.

After a few moments of silence, I said, "Do you need any help?"

"No. Thanks for the iced tea."

I rose from the grass and went inside, feeling terrible about how I had handled the whole thing, and realized I had damaged Mia's trust. She had every right to be mad at me. As I sat at the table, fearing the worst, she came in through the garage, took off her shoes, and approached me.

She said, "Look, I'm not going to make a big deal out of this because I understand your reasoning. But you have to know that for our relationship to work, it has to be based on trust and truth. I view keeping something from me the same as lying to me, and that just won't work."

Relieved, I said, "I understand completely and agree—I apologize. Thanks for cutting me some slack this time." I reached out to her and hugged her waist, my head on her belly.

She ran her fingers through my hair and said, "I'm going up to shower, then I'll see what we have for dinner."

While she was upstairs, I remained at the table, feeling thankful she had forgiven me. A few minutes later, I called Hannah. After hello's, I said, "I'm going to back off the case, Han. I don't think you need to worry about it for now."

"You scared Mom and me half to death, Dad. I'm okay with it, but Mom is pissed."

"I can imagine. I'll call her now, but just stay alert, and let me know if you see anything odd."

"Okay. Thanks for letting me know."

"Bye, Han. I love you!"

Next, I called Sheila.

When she answered, I said, "I wanted to let you know that I've stopped working the case I was on. They have successfully scared me off, and there should be nothing more to be concerned about."

"Christ, Dan. You can't be doing things that endanger your family."

"I agree. That's why I backed off. Just keep your eyes open and set the alarm."

"Okay."

CHAPTER 16

On the second Monday in April, the District Attorney in White Plains held a press conference, shown live on the 5:00 news. He announced that while Officers O'Riley and Maddox had been fired, there was insufficient evidence to charge them with a crime. Mia and I watched in disbelief. By 6:30, protestors were gathering at City Hall. By 8:00, riots had broken out, and windows were being broken. The Police were out in force setting up barricades and trying to send the rioters home. A half-hour later, a police car was tipped over and set on fire. We watched as the whole thing unfolded on live TV until we could no longer stay awake. I assumed I would be hearing from Seth in the morning.

The following day, I woke to thunderstorms. I quietly slipped into the bathroom so as not to wake Mia. After my morning routine, I dressed for the day, went downstairs, and started the coffee. While it was brewing, I opened my phone, and sure enough, there was a text from Seth. He asked if I could come by in the afternoon and suggested I watch TV this morning. After my first sip, I turned on the local news.

They were focused on last night's riots, which continued into the early morning hours and were only broken up by the heavy rain that had moved in overnight. The anchor said the Jordan family's attorney would make a statement at 10:00 a.m. As the news continued, they replayed a continuous loop of the riots and the weather forecast for the next few hours. Mia was equally fascinated by last night's events when she joined me. As promised, Seth appeared at the top of the hour at a podium inside City Hall in a room large enough to handle the media.

"Good morning, ladies and gentlemen. The Jordan family has asked me to thank you all for covering this incomprehensible decision by the District Attorney. Never before have I seen a clearer case of murder than what happened to Jerome Jordan a month ago. This morning, I filed a civil suit against the City of White Plains, the Police Department, and both Officers involved. While we can't impose a prison sentence, we intend to hold them accountable for this egregious crime and compensate the Jordan family for the loss of their cherished son. I have time for a few questions."

We watched as chaos ensued, with reporters clamoring to have their questions heard. When order was restored, Seth could select who would ask a question. This went on for twenty minutes, with the common theme of how the DA could not have charged the officers. Seth claimed he was just as dumbfounded as the reporters and spoke about Officer O'Riley's violent history that the department allowed to continue.

In closing, he said, "If the White Plains Police Department had removed Officer O'Riley from the line of duty as his previous conduct called for, Jerome Jordan would be alive today."

Questions were still being yelled as Seth left the room, but once he was gone, the reporters gathered their things and hurried off to post their stories.

After turning off the TV, Mia and I remained at the table, watching the rain pour down, obscuring our view of the Sound. Later, I headed to Seth's office with the wipers on high speed as huge puddles tugged on the steering wheel. Once there, Paula and I briefly discussed the last twenty-four hours before Seth welcomed me into his office.

"I'm bringing in another attorney I know from law school to help me with this case. There will be too many briefs and motions to be filed for me to handle by myself. I'd like to have you involved in our strategy sessions a couple of times each week if you're willing to resume working on it," he offered.

"I'd like to be involved if we can ensure the safety of the people I care about."

"I have already engaged security people to protect Paula, her family, and myself. As I said before, I can also provide them for your family."

"I'll need to figure that out. I'm sure Iona University doesn't want a bodyguard hanging out at her dorm. Maybe if she moved in with her mother, we can have one there."

"We'll assign two, one for each of them. One can drive your daughter to school and remain with her at all times, and the other can protect your ex-wife."

"Okay. I'll have to consult them first, of course."

"I understand. Let me know as soon as you can."

"There is also a woman I've been living with. I doubt anyone knows about her yet, but if I'm being followed, It's only a matter of time.'

"We can assign someone to her if you like and also someone for you."

"This will be some expensive security detail!"

"Like I said, the money has been pouring in, and this security company has the personnel to handle it."

"Okay, I'll confirm all this with you tomorrow. Assuming I'm in, what's my first assignment?"

"Let's determine if we should rule out Officer Maddox from murder charges. If he is only guilty of supporting his senior partner, we won't waste any effort on him. After that, I want to look into O'Riley's superiors, who let him get away with this behavior for all these years. I'll subpoena the records and see who was responsible."

"Okay, I think I have a picture of what you need."

"Great. I look forward to speaking with you tomorrow."

We rose from our seats and shook hands as I left his office. Once I rode the elevator down to the lobby, I called Sheila's cell.

"Hello, Dan."

"Hi. Might you have time today to meet with Hannah and me?"

"Is this about her safety?"

"Yes. Hers, mine, and yours."

"This sounds serious. I'm already home from work and available anytime."

"Good. I'll call Hannah and let you know what time works for her."

"Okay."

When I called Hannah, I got her voicemail and left a message that I wanted to have a family meeting with her and her mother this afternoon. When I stepped outside, the rain had diminished to a drizzle. After reaching the car, Hannah returned my call.

"Hi, Dad. What's going on?"

Trying to sound unconcerned, I said, "I want to speak to you and your mother about my being followed last week."

"I just finished my last class for the day. Anytime works for me."

"Good, I'll pick you up in a half hour."

"Okay, Dad. I'll be under the porch in front of the dorm."

I called Sheila back and told her we would arrive within the hour. While driving, I called Mia to let her know what was happening and told her we would speak more tonight. She told me she was making shrimp scampi for dinner. *What did I do to deserve this woman?*

The rain had begun to ease, and when Hannah was in the car, I explained that I needed to work on the case again because the DA had failed to bring murder charges, and there would be no investigation. She said everyone in school was discussing the case and the riots, and she understood my thinking. I hoped her mother would, too.

Sheila and Hannah hugged as we entered the house, then she led us to the kitchen, where the news was on TV. After she muted it, we discussed Jerome's death and the events of last night and this morning. When I explained my role in the investigation, Hannah was supportive.

"Why do you feel it is your duty to right all the wrongs in this world?" Sheila asked while looking me square in the eye.

Hannah put her hand on my forearm.

"It's what I do, Sheila. I solve crimes, not all the wrongs in the world."

"Even if it endangers your family?"

"I have a plan for that. I'm working for the Jordan family's attorney. They're well-funded and will provide security for anyone who needs it. We think Hannah should move back home, and we'll assign two armed security guards, one for each of you. One can drive Hannah to her classes and be with her all day. The other can protect you here, at work, or wherever you go."

Her attitude brightened after I explained the plan to keep them safe. "Are you cool with this, Hannah?" she asked.

"I am, Mom. I graduate in a few weeks and will be moving back home anyway."

"Okay, Dan. I'm willing to give it a try. Will these security guards be male or female?" Sheila asked.

"I'll try to have at least one female assigned," I replied.

When they seemed satisfied, I asked, "Would you like to return to your dorm tonight, Hannah?"

"I have to. All my things are there."

"Fine, I'll drive you back. Hopefully, I can get the security guards here tomorrow afternoon, and I'll pick you up after classes then."

"Sure, that should work."

"Thank you both for putting up with this. I hope it's not too much of a burden," I said as Hannah and I rose to leave.

We all hugged at the door, and I thanked Sheila for cooperating.

After dropping Hannah off at her dorm, I headed for Mia's with my eyes glued to the mirror. I found myself clenching my hands and grinding my teeth—the pressure of my family being threatened had gotten to me. I wondered how it had reached this point, but I thought back and realized it had gradually built, one step at a time, little by little. There was no longer room for a mistake.

I told Mia about the day's events over cocktails before dinner. I explained that I intended to stay on the boat so they wouldn't learn about her and that we could provide a security guard for her if needed.

"You mean have a guard stay here with me all the time?"

"Yes, they would probably rotate a team of two," I replied.

"Judy wants me to spend a few weeks in Portugal with her—a sisters' trip.

Maybe I should give in and say yes."

"That would work, too."

"I'll call her later and see what she has in mind."

Mia's scampi dinner was marvelous. She had stuffed butterflied jumbo shrimp with a mixture of butter, garlic, shallots, parsley, and breadcrumbs and baked them, melting the garlic butter. She told me she learned the recipe at a cooking class in Florence. Along with a Caesar salad and fresh bread to soak up the scampi sauce, we overdosed on garlic while enjoying a bottle of Muscadet.

The following morning, I searched Officer Maddox's file for anything I could follow up on. He only had fifteen months of service with the department and just one previous patrol partner. Before making calls, I went out to purchase a cheap pre-paid burner phone that looked like an old Motorola flip phone. When I returned to Mia's, I called the WPPD and asked for Officer Danzinger. When he came on the line, I told him I was investigating for the Jordan family's attorney and wanted to know more about John Maddox. Surprisingly, he was eager to speak with me.

"I was John's partner when he first joined the force. We rode together for a year, and my job was to teach him the ropes. I was shocked to hear he was involved with the Jordan kid. He never showed a violent side the whole time I was with him. Just the opposite; he always tried to do the right thing."

"Did you have any contact with him after this incident?"

"We spoke after roll call one morning, and he told me how ashamed he was. The next day, he was suspended, and I haven't seen him since."

"Have you any experience with Sean O'Riley?"

Shaking his head, he said, "He's an old-timer who never advanced and always walks around like a bull with his chest out. I was never partnered with him, but he seemed content with just going on patrol each day. I know he's been suspended before for similar incidents."

"Is there anything else you'd like me to know?"

"Not really, just that John has a young wife and child. I hope the courts don't treat him too harshly."

"Thanks so much for your time today, Officer."

"No problem."

I made notes of the conversation and then attempted to call Officer Scully. I was told he was out on patrol, so I left the burner phone number for a callback. I resumed my search of the police files, looking for the names of superiors to whom they would have both answered. Besides Detective Kidd, I found a Sergeant Bruno. After calling the department again, he came on the line, and I greeted him like I had Officer Danzinger. His response was completely different. He said, "No comment," and hung up.

Later that morning, I received a text from Seth confirming that a male and a female security guard would arrive at Sheila's house at 4:00 for duty twenty- four hours a day with rotating rest periods. I called

Sheila and Hannah and made plans to pick up Hannah and deliver her to the house mid-afternoon.

After lunch, I received a call back from Officer Scully on the burner phone.

While he wasn't as friendly as Officer Danzinger, he was at least willing to answer my questions regarding John Maddox. He told me that he, too, was surprised at John's involvement with the Jordan stop and had never seen a violent side to him. When asked about Sean O'Riley, he said he had no interaction with him, and even if he had, he wouldn't speak negatively about a fellow cop. This was the sort of response I expected all along.

After ending the call, I realized that the burner phone could also be traced with repeated use, so I decided not to make any more calls with either phone from Mia's house. After sending Seth a lengthy email summarizing the day's interviews, I headed to Iona.

When I arrived at Hannah's dorm, she had her clothes in a couple of suitcases and her school stuff in a few boxes. We loaded it all into the Grand Cherokee and headed for home. As we neared the quiet residential neighborhood of modest colonial and Cape-Cod-style homes, memories of Hannah playing hopscotch in the street and growing up with her friends came flooding back. I pictured her in pig-tails with a colorful bandage on her knee.

Once inside Sheila's house, I met with the security people and discovered they were both recently retired military. I watched her body language while we chatted in the kitchen, and she seemed comfortable with who we sent to protect them.

Frank Wright had served twenty years with the Marines. He was fit and wore his hair in a flat top with short sidewalls—exactly how I would picture a forty-five-year-old ex-Marine. His specialty was cyber-security, but he was between assignments and available for this duty. Kristine Wallace was in her twenties, with brown eyes and short sandy-blonde hair. She appeared to be a bit of a tomboy. She had just completed her four-year stint in the Army to qualify for a paid college education. She planned to attend NYU in the fall.

We exchanged contact information, and I left it up to Hannah and Sheila to decide who would be assigned to whom. Or maybe they would rotate; it was up to them.

I headed to Mia's on an indirect route, stopping occasionally to watch for a tail. Seeing none, I continued to her house.

Once inside, Mia and I hugged, and I made a batch of cosmopolitans, a change of pace for us. We sat in our happy place overlooking the water, sipping our drinks. While it was cloudy, we could still see Long Island clearly. Knowing it was her day at the Humane Society, I asked how it went.

"We got a whole litter of puppies in today; eight of them, just a few weeks old. They're probably mixed breed, but they look like German Shepherds."

"I'll bet that's a rare occasion."

"Maybe like once a year—they are so adorable. You should see all of them rolled up in a ball—it's the cutest thing ever!"

"Isn't that too young to be apart from the mother?"

"It is. We'll have to bottle-feed them for another few weeks. I'm going in tomorrow to do that."

Sensing her excitement, I said, "You're going to want to bring one home, aren't you?"

"I'd love to bring one home, but raising a puppy is a big commitment. I'm sure we'll find a home for all of them. No one can resist these puppies."

I pulled her close and kissed her forehead. It was great to see her happy, and it took my mind off my troubles. This time with Mia was the best part of my day—by far—and after thinking about that a bit, I realized how important she had become in my life.

When we finished our drinks, we went to the kitchen, where she had made a pot of potato-leek soup, the first thing she had ever served me. We enjoyed it with some crusty bread, then returned to our happy place, where we fell asleep in each other's arms. At some point, we must have climbed the stairs to her bedroom.

CHAPTER 17

When I awoke, I heard Mia on the elliptical machine in the other room and saw a text from Seth asking if I could attend a strategy meeting at 10:00. I confirmed I would be there.

After dressing, I went to the kitchen, poured myself a coffee, and put some strawberries and yogurt in bowls. Soon after, Mia joined me for breakfast with a towel around her neck.

"Good morning. I see you worked up a glow this morning," I smiled.

"Thanks for not calling it a sweat!" she laughed.

We enjoyed breakfast with one another before I headed to White Plains.

When I entered the office, Paula introduced me to Linda Cole, the new attorney Seth hired. She appeared to be about thirty, attractive, with styled and highlighted brown hair and wearing a skirt suit that fit her perfectly. She had eyebrows that most women would kill for and appeared quite competent. After we shook hands, she explained that she had attended law school with Seth, and they had dated a few times. When a relationship never evolved, they remained friends and have stayed in touch ever since.

I noticed a new desk alongside Paula's and assumed it would be hers. While we chatted, Paula set out water, coffee, and pastries in the glass-walled conference room. A moment later, Seth exited his inner office and said, "Good, I see you two have met. Shall we get this party started?"

The three of us entered the conference room, followed by Paula after she set up the phones to go to voicemail. I settled in with a legal pad and my case file in front of me while Paula and Linda opened their laptops.

Seth said, "Let's start by reviewing Dan's interviews with the police associates of O'Riley and Maddox. Dan?"

"Okay, I'll start in the order I did the interviews,"

I recalled the conversations using my email reports as a guide. They asked questions from time to time, but within an hour, I was able to go through all my notes in detail. I concluded with my conversation with Anne Gibbs, the psychologist I had spoken to.

When I finished, Seth asked, "Does everyone agree that we shouldn't waste any further effort on John Maddox?"

We all nodded in agreement.

"Dan, are you still being followed?" Seth asked.

"Well, I just resumed my investigation yesterday, but I assume they'll be back at it."

"Okay, we should know soon enough if they resume. Linda, where are we on the filings?"

"Everything's in order with the initial filings. Judge Marchant has been assigned the case, and his reputation is as a fair, down-the-middle judge who follows the law. Most of his decisions have held up on appeal. I would think he would elect a jury trial in this case," Linda concluded.

"I agree," Seth confirmed. "I assume they'll have multiple defense attorneys. Do we know who any of them are yet?"

"Not yet. I'm sure O'Riley will have his own, supplied by the union. The city has not announced who they will use yet."

"Probably Marshall Green. He seems to get all the work from City Hall," Seth said.

"Regardless, I'm ready for the initial motions, but we'll need to subpoena testimony from everyone Dan has spoken to and interview Anne Gibbs to see if she's the right psychologist for us to use. If so, she'll need to do a complete workup on Sean O'Riley," Linda said.

Seth continued, "Dan, are there any other cops on your list to interview?"

"I've interviewed everyone John Maddox was partnered with, everyone involved with Sean O'Riley's suspensions, and a few of his direct superiors. That's all in my reports. I can keep at it and go back further if you'd like," I offered.

"How about we start looking into some of the higher-ups that signed off to reinstate O'Riley after all these suspensions? Captains and Chiefs."

"I can do that. I assume you're willing to subpoena anyone involved?"

"Yes. If they have direct involvement or testimony beneficial to our case."

"Got it," I concluded.

"Anything else?" Seth asked.

Paula and Linda had been typing away on their laptops the whole time.

They both shook their heads, No, and continued typing.

"Okay, this is a good start. Thank you all," Seth said as he rose from his seat. We all filed out and shook hands before I left the office.

Once I reached my car, I reviewed the case files again to see who was involved with O'Riley's reinstatements. I could see who signed off, and from the dates, I could research who the Captains and Chiefs were at the time. I drove to the office I shared with Jim to make calls on the burner phone. As I pulled out of the parking garage, a Ford Mustang followed me out.

The direct route to Scarsdale was straight down Route 22. It would be a slow drive with all the lights, but it allowed me to see if the Mustang was tailing me. He dropped back a few cars but drove through a yellow light to keep up. I pulled into a Wendy's parking lot and saw him continue past. When I resumed my route south, the Mustang did not reappear, but the black Explorer did.

I smiled. So they had bumped up their game to a two-car tail. I pulled into the next gas station and stayed near the road to get the plate number as the Explorer drove past. BY4-779, a New York plate. I resumed my route south, this time behind him. The windows were tinted dark, so I couldn't identify the driver, but I was sure it was a man. When I reached the office and saw that Jim was out, I called Frosty.

"Detective Frost."

"Hi, Matt. Can you run a plate number for me?"

"What, not even a 'Hello! How are you?'"

I laughed. We caught up with each other's lives for a minute before I told him the tail had resumed and that I had security guards for Hannah and Sheila at the house.

"Okay, what's the plate number?"

I repeated it, and he told me he'd get right back to me. I then resumed looking through the case files, making notes of who to call, and looking up who the higher-ups were at the time.

Ten minutes later, Frosty called. "It appears that plate is registered to Billy the Kid," he laughed.

"Billy the Kid?"

"The black Explorer is registered to a William Kidd of Hartsdale."

"Interesting. He's with the WPPD and was O'Riley's partner during one of his previous violent incidents."

"I guess that tells you who his pals are."

"Yup, thanks for this, buddy. Today, they graduated to a two-car tail."

"Even more interesting. You did the right thing with the security guards. Where are you sleeping?"

"I'll be back on the boat. I don't want to be tracked to Mia's; at least the docks are gated."

"Anyone who can manage a two-car tail should have no trouble with a marina gate."

"Yeah, I know. Maybe I need a security guard, too. Do you want to come by the marina for a beer this afternoon?"

"Sure, I'll see you shortly after 5:00."

Now that I had elected to stay on the boat, I called Mia. "Hello, love. How's your day going?"

"Fine, sweetheart," I replied. I told her about the tail resuming and explained why I wouldn't be coming tonight. I asked if she had spoken to Judy about Portugal.

After expressing disappointment that she wouldn't see me, she said, "I spoke with her about it this morning. She's looking into a short-term rental house in the Algarve."

"I hear it's lovely there in the springtime."

"Yes, I've been looking online. Maybe we should go sooner rather than later."

"I would feel better having you out of the country until this blows over."

"Okay, I'll let Judy know to push up the schedule. When will I see you?"

"I'll figure out something. I just don't want to be followed to your house."

"Maybe I can come to the boat?"

"Maybe. Frosty is stopping by later to scope out the marina security."

"Good, I'll let you know what Judy comes up with."

"Okay, Mia. Love you."

"Love you, too."

By the time Jim returned to the office, I had resumed reviewing the case files and brought him up to date with the last few days' events. He was happy to hear that Hannah was back home with twenty-four-hour security now that they had resumed following me. He offered to help break up the tail for me, and we discussed some ideas for doing that. After completing my time log for the week, I headed to the marina to meet Frosty.

The Mustang was back on my tail, and once again, he did not follow me over the bridge onto City Island. I guessed either he knew where I was going or didn't want to get trapped on the single road that dead-ended on the island.

Once in the parking lot, I walked around the car, looking underneath it for a tracking device. Sure enough, a magnetic case was inside the left front wheel well. Again, I smiled to myself. Knowing of its existence, it would be my choice to allow them to track me or not. Or, I could devise a plan to throw them off my tail at the most opportune time.

When aboard Privateer, I opened all the hatches, turned on some old Doobie Brothers tunes, and sat in the cockpit surveying the marina. It wasn't long before I saw Frosty coming down the ramp with a small brown paper bag. After I opened the gate for him, he pulled out a pack of Guinness pint-sized cans with the thing inside that makes them foam when poured into a glass. After returning to the boat, we did precisely that, and after a sip or two, I could understand why this was his beverage of choice.

After touching our pint glasses, I told him about discovering the tracking device.

"Let's take a walk around this place and analyze the security. Can we bring the beers?"

"Sure," I replied.

We climbed off the boat, being careful not to spill our beers. Our first stop was the security gate with a five-foot-high chain-link fence on both sides. We could easily imagine someone climbing over the fence with nothing more than a stool. A similar gate and fence led to the marina office at the other end of the main dock, with the same ease of defeating. When glancing over the rest of the marina, we immediately saw that anyone with a rowboat could come in by water and have free access to the entire marina. Not good! We then inspected the video surveillance, which consisted of a camera at each finger dock and another at each gate.

Frosty asked, "Are these cameras monitored in real time?"

"No. They record on a loop, recording over themselves every forty-eight hours."

"So someone could come in here on a rowboat, murder you on Friday night, and if no one found you by Sunday night, there would be no account of what happened?"

I paused and said, "I guess that's about right."

"This surveillance is here to prevent vandalism. Nothing more." Frosty's hard factual observations were depressing. I walked back to Privateer with my head down as he followed. Once aboard, I said, "I guess I'll need a night watchman. Otherwise, I won't be able to sleep."

"A night watchman would be good," he agreed.

I was surprised at myself for assuming the marina was somewhat secure. I had the same ability as Frosty to analyze the situation, so it must have been wishful thinking to feel safe here. After another Guinness and more discussion about security, Frosty headed home for dinner with his family. I called Hannah.

"Hi, Dad."

"Hey. How's it going with Frank and Kristine?"

"All good. Kristine has the spare bedroom, and Frank sleeps on a cot in the TV room."

"How's your mom handling it?"

"Mom seems fine with it; she even asked him what he likes for dinner."

"Good to hear. Which one is driving you to school?"

"Kristine. She's interested in learning about campus life, and I think we're becoming friends."

"I assume Frank is driving your Mother to work?"

"Yes."

"Okay. Keep your eyes open."

"Will do, Dad. Good night."

After another dinner alone, I had a poor night's sleep, again with my gun next to me and with my ears focused on every little sound.

CHAPTER 18

While my coffee was brewing, I texted Seth that I would need overnight security at the marina. He immediately replied that he would arrange it. After my first few sips, I took out my notes from yesterday and made a plan for the day.

When I researched who the higher-ups were at WPPD over the last dozen years, I found just one police chief: James Allen, who served from 2008 until now. There were quite a few Captains who served over that time. After listing them all, I reconciled the names that appeared anywhere in O'Riley's service record, which narrowed it down to five, and then determined which were still active, leaving two: Captains Johnson and Owens. That's where I would start.

Since whoever was following me knew I lived on the boat, I saw no reason not to use the burner phone from the marina. On my first call to the WPPD, I asked for Captain Johnson. The person answering the phone asked what the call was regarding, and after telling him I was calling from Attorney Bodner's office, he told me Captain Johnson was unavailable, but I could leave a message. I left the burner phone number, and before ending the call, I asked to speak with Captain Owens. The response was the same, and I asked if he could also return my call.

An hour later, my cell phone rang. The caller identified himself as Detective Crocker from Manhattan North.

"Good morning, Detective. What can I do for you?"

"I have some off-the-record information for you. Can I trust you to forget where you heard it?"

"Yes. I'll agree to that."

"There is a group of white supremacists within the WPPD, and O'Riley is one of them."

"Can you tell me their names?"

"I can, but I won't. I can tell you there are a half dozen of them, ranking all the way up to Captain."

"Is there anything else you can tell me?"

"I never witnessed this myself, but I was aware of contests they had where points were given for arresting or beating up a Black or Hispanic guy. Or woman, for that matter. Then they got together once a month to celebrate and give out awards."

"It was that organized?"

"Yeah. I'm telling you this because when I heard the DA didn't charge them with murder, I could no longer keep it to myself."

"Thanks for the tip, Detective. It will give me a new direction to work."

"I was hoping it would," he said before ending the call.

I took a deep breath and sat back in the salon to digest what I had just learned. You would imagine this sort of thing still going on in the Deep South, but not in suburban New York. With images of Jerome's beating running through my head, I couldn't help but imagine other instances of this group's activities.

Before long, I felt the need to share this with Seth.

"Good morning, Dan. A security guard will contact you shortly and can start duty tonight," he said.

"Thanks for that. You won't believe what I just found out."

"Try me."

I went on to disclose the entire conversation with Detective Crocker, making sure he understood the confidentiality and closing with my disbelief that it was occurring in White Plains.

"That might help explain why the DA didn't press charges; he must have known of the group and didn't want that information to get out."

"Can you imagine the public reaction? They would call for the Chief's head and an investigation of the entire department," I said.

"Can you come in for a team meeting this afternoon? This information will alter our case strategy."

"Sure, I can be there at 1:00."

"Great, I'll have Paula send out for lunch."

"See you then."

When I entered Seth's office, he, Linda, and Paula were already in the conference room passing out sandwiches. They looked at me in awe for providing the new information.

Linda was the first to ask, "How did you learn about a white supremacist group of cops right here in White Plains?"

"From a former cop who used to work there."

"Is he willing to testify?"

"Probably not. He gave me the information strictly off the record, and I promised to forget where it came from."

"This changes our whole focus. We need to identify the other members and get one to testify," Seth said.

"Sounds like more work for me. Any suggestions where I start?" I asked.

Everyone shook their heads and remained quiet while focused on their lunch. Paula was the first to speak. "Can we find out if anyone besides O'Riley was suspended for violence?"

"I can subpoena the records of other similar cases. I'll need to be specific, however. Otherwise, they'll just say we're fishing, and a judge won't grant the subpoena," Seth said.

"How about limiting it to cases where the victims were non-white, and an investigation took place?" Linda suggested.

"That could be worth a try," Seth conceded.

I said, "Of all the cops I contacted, a few were immediate 'No comments.' I can start looking deeper into those. I ran the plate on the black Explorer that was following me. It's registered to one of them—William Kidd."

"Then that's certainly where to start," Seth said.

"How about I search for newspaper stories of incidents involving the police and Blacks or Hispanics?" Paula said.

"Good idea, Paula. Let's get to work," Seth concluded.

As I pulled out of the parking garage, the Mustang appeared in my mirror. I assume he knew my location from the tracker. As I headed south on Route 22, I called Jim.

"Hi, Dan."

"Hey, buddy. I'm being followed again. Are you at the office by chance?"

"I am."

"How about I lead him past the office, and you tuck in behind him? I'll stop abruptly, and you pinch him in. We'll confront him."

"Sure. Are you armed?"

"I have a piece."

"Good. I'll be armed, too."

"Okay, Jim. It's a late-model gold Mustang. We'll be south-bound, ETA about ten minutes."

"I'll be waiting."

As I continued driving, my excitement level rose. I hoped to have the Mustang close to me so other cars would not be involved. A few minutes later, just one car was between us on the four-lane road. As I approached the office, I slowed enough to cause the car between us to pass me, leaving the Mustang directly behind. When we passed the office, I saw Jim's Highlander pull out behind the Mustang. With our spacing now perfect, I jammed on the brakes, forcing the Mustang to do the same. Jim stopped just inches from his bumper, leaving him no room to maneuver. Even though this was a busy area, I got out and approached the Mustang driver's window with the gun in my jacket pocket and rapped on the glass. Jim went to the passenger side and did the same.

When the windows came down, the driver said, "Hey, what the fuck are you doing? I'm a cop!"

"No. You used to be a cop, Sean O'Riley. What do you think you will accomplish by following me?" I saw that Jim had his gun inside the vehicle pointed at O'Riley so that a passerby wouldn't see it.

"I don't mean any harm; I'm just trying to scare you off," O'Riley said. "That's not going to happen, O'Riley. We're going to see you go down for the murder of Jerome Jordan."

When he didn't reply, Jim and I returned to our vehicles and drove away, leaving O'Riley behind to stew. We returned to the office, reliving what had just occurred and speculating about his response.

When I told Jim about the white supremacist group at WPPD, he was just as surprised as I had been.

"He's a loose cannon," Jim said. "There's no way to know how far he'll go to save himself or other group members."

"If he were smart, he'd leave the country and never return."

"Yeah, but he's not smart. Does he have a wife and family?"

"Divorced; no kids," I replied.

"Do we know who any other members of the group are?"

"My guess is Detective Kidd is one of them. The Ford Explorer that was following me is registered to him."

"This is getting more interesting by the minute. What are Seth's plans?"

"He wants to identify the other group members and get one to flip."

"That makes sense," Jim concluded.

Before Jim left for the day, he removed two tracking devices from his bottom drawer, placed them on my desk, and said, "Here, take these in case you want to track the trackers."

"Good idea. Thanks," I said and put them in my jacket pocket.

I called Frank Wright, the security guard at Sheila's. I told him about my confrontation with O'Riley and asked him to be on heightened alert in case he retaliated. I also shared the info on the vehicles that had tailed me. He sounded very competent.

I then called Mia to see how her travel plans were coming along. When she answered, just her voice made me want to see her. I wondered what she was wearing and asked her what room of the house she was in.

"That's an odd question," she replied.

"I'm trying to picture where you are and what you're wearing. I miss you."

"I'm lying in bed naked, rubbing body oil all over myself. Is that the image you were hoping for?"

"It is. Can I help with the oil?"

She laughed, "Not to destroy your fantasy, but I'm in the kitchen standing over the stove in yoga pants and a 'Save the Earth' T-shirt."

"That's still a good image. How are your travel plans coming?"

"We leave tomorrow evening, flying to Lisbon, where we'll stay at the Four Seasons for a week. Then we'll rent a car and drive to Lagos, where a house is rented for two weeks. I'll send you a link to the rental."

"That sounds fantastic. When were you going to tell me?"

"It was just confirmed this morning, and I assumed you'd call today. Can we see each other tonight?"

"I'll figure out a way to get there come hell or high water."

"Wonderful. I'll dress for the occasion."

"My goodness, you're killing me, Mia."

"That's my intent. See you then, lover."

With images of Mia in my head, any thought of doing more work that day went out the window, and I headed to the Marina to shower before going to her house. After traveling a few blocks, I noticed the Explorer once again behind me, a few cars back. I assumed Billy the Kidd had spoken with O'Riley at some point and resumed the tail despite me being on to them. Once again, when I crossed the bridge onto City Island, he continued on.

Shortly after boarding the boat, I received an incoming call. "This is Dave Culver calling for Dan Burnett."

"This is Dan."

"I'm calling from Westchester Security; I'm your night watchman."

"Yes, thanks for calling, Dave. Actually, it would be best if you didn't start until tomorrow. Is that okay?"

"Sure, no problem."

"How about we meet at the Marina at six p.m.? I'll buy you dinner, and we'll review the job."

"I'll be there at six."

"You'll need to call me when you arrive so I can let you in and give you a key card."

"Got it. See you then."

An hour later, when I was showered and dressed, I went to my car and removed the tracking device. I stuck it in the bushes where I could find it again when I didn't mind being followed. While driving to Mamaroneck, I saw no one following, even after exiting and re-entering the highway.

Mia greeted me at the door in her silky robe with a passionate kiss. From the way her nipples danced against the fabric, I knew she was wearing nothing underneath. I followed her to our happy place, in front of the glass doors, where she had an open bottle of champagne on ice. After a few sips, we resumed kissing, my hand exploring inside her robe. When we couldn't take it any longer, we carried the champagne upstairs and made love for the rest of the afternoon.

Eventually, we went downstairs for dinner, which was in the oven, keeping warm. She had prepared veal osso buco with braised root vegetables, one of my all-time favorite meals. As she plated our dinner, I opened a bottle of Montepulciano, poured two glasses, and sat down to eat.

"This is fabulous. What did I ever do to deserve a woman like you?"

"I don't know. Maybe the question should be, *'How were we so lucky to have found each other and get a second chance at love at this time in our lives?'*"

I leaned across the table and kissed her, savoring her lush lips, realizing how much I would miss her.

After finishing dinner and clearing the table, we returned to the living room with our wine glasses, gazing at the night sky and cuddling together on the couch. Aware this would be our last evening together for a few weeks, we relished every moment.

I was awoken the next morning by the light touch of Mia's fingernails on my chest and belly. It wasn't long before she had achieved her goal and mounted me with her breasts hovering over my face. When I lifted my head to kiss them, she teased me by pinning my shoulders and raising up to keep them out of reach. Eventually, she relented, and our passion overwhelmed us. The next few minutes were pure animal lust, rising to a crescendo and leaving us spent.

When our breathing and heart rate had returned to normal, she whispered, "That should keep me content the whole time I'm away."

"Me, too," I laughed.

After breakfast, she walked me to the door, and we clung to one another, not wanting to part. Eventually, I said, "Well, you have packing to do, and I have work. Maybe I should go."

"Okay, love. I'll call you from the airport."

"Yes, please do," I said, walking out the door. I looked back for one last image of her before driving away.

CHAPTER 19

Once aboard Privateer, I opened the Jordan case file, which soon became scattered across the table. When a file becomes this thick and unruly, it's time to put it in a binder. I took out my three-hole punch and created a book with all the notes and documents in chronological order. It took a while, but I now felt organized.

This was how I learned to conduct an investigation. Every day or two, I would review the case book to determine what I knew and what I didn't know. Then, after listing all the things I didn't know, I would focus on those. After doing this repeatedly, I would eventually know it all.

Today, my focus was on identifying members of the supremacist group. I was sure Detective Kidd was one because he was tailing me. Reviewing my notes from my last conversation with Detective Crocker, I knew a Captain was involved. At least one. That's where I would start. Assuming neither Captain Johnson nor Captain Owens would return my call, I elected to go on the offensive and follow one of them. But first, I'd need to know about their vehicles.

I called Frosty at the 49th precinct. "Detective Frost."

"Hi, Matt. It's Dan."

"How's it going, pal."

"Pretty good. If I give you two names, can you find out their vehicle registrations?"

"Sure. Ready when you are," he said.

After giving him the names, I told him they were both Captains with the WPPD.

"Nothing like going after the top of the food chain," he laughed.

"This is getting more interesting by the day, Matt. I'll tell you all about it next time I see you."

"Okay, I'll get on it right now."

"Thanks, Frosty."

Less than an hour later, he called back.

"Okay, here's what we have. James Johnson drives a 2019 Chevy Tahoe, white, with the NY tag 745-EYC. Douglas Owens has two registered cars: a 2022 Dodge Ram pick-up, silver with the NY tag HUNTER, and a 1971 Corvette, red with the NY tag MY-VET. Both Johnson and Owens reside in Scarsdale.

After writing it all down, I said, "A vanity plate guy, huh?"

"Sounds like it."

"Thanks for this, Matt. We'll get together soon for beers on me."

"Okay, but be careful out there."

"Always."

Before leaving, I thought about what to do with the tracking device. If I left it in the bushes, they might figure out I had discovered it. But if I put it back under the car, they could follow me as I attempted to follow one of the Captains.

I didn't like either option, but when I reached the parking lot, I saw a produce delivery truck alongside the diner. I took the tracker and stuck it under the truck's body. They'd figure it out after a while, but I'd have fun knowing they'd be chasing a produce truck around for most of the day.

As I drove to White Plains, there was no sign of anyone following me. After parking on the street near the police station, I walked around back to their gated parking lot, looking for any of the vehicles that Frosty had identified. Along the back row, I saw the Ram truck with the HUNTER license plate. After scouting the area, I found a place to park outside the lot's exit with a good line of sight. I returned to my car, moved it to the new spot, and settled in to wait it out.

While biding my time, I also noticed the black Explorer that had followed me was parked in the lot as well. An hour later, I saw two men approach the Explorer and stand alongside it, talking for a few minutes. I recognized the bloated face of Detective Kidd. The other guy was younger and had dark hair and a well-trimmed full beard. I took a few pictures before Kidd got in the Explorer and drove off; the other guy climbed into a Chrysler 300 and followed. I briefly thought about tailing them but knew Kidd would surely identify my Grand Cherokee behind him, so I stayed put after noting the tag on the Chrysler.

Ten minutes later, a cop in uniform with captain's stripes got into the Ram pickup and drove out. I followed, keeping a car or two between us for about fifteen minutes through a rural area, and watched as he pulled into a roadside bar and grill. As I drove past, I saw the Explorer and the Chrysler parked in front. A half mile later, I turned around, returned, and parked across the road at an Agway store. From there, I had a clear view of the comings and goings of the bar and grill. As I settled in for the wait, I saw O'Riley arrive in the Mustang and enter the establishment. Realizing my stroke of luck, I took out my phone and adjusted the camera settings for a close-up of the door when they came out.

While waiting, I called Frosty and asked him to run the plate on the Chrysler. He said he was not at the station but would get back to me later in the afternoon. After waiting for an hour, the Roadhouse door opened, and four of them exited together laughing, followed by O'Riley and two others working on toothpicks. I started taking pictures of all seven of them together and continued as they drove off, getting good shots of each person and each vehicle. This felt like a clandestine meeting, and I wondered if I had just witnessed one of their monthly awards meetings. With the photo evidence in my pocket, I drove to Seth's office to share it with them after letting Paula know I was on my way.

They were anxious to see what I had when I entered the office. The four of us sat around the conference table, and I AirDropped them the photos.

As we individually examined them, they realized their importance as evidence. "I recognize O'Riley. Who are the others?" Seth said.

"The one in uniform is Captain Owens. Detective Kidd is the one who's driving the Explorer. I should know who was driving the Chrysler this afternoon, and I don't know the others."

Linda asked, "Do you think this was a planned group meeting?"

"Judging from the cast of characters, it has to be."

"These are great shots, Dan. We'll start by subpoenaing their records," Seth said.

Just then, my phone vibrated, and I saw it was Frosty. "What do you have for me, Matt?"

"The Chrysler is registered to a Nicolas Bruno of Tarrytown."

"Thanks, pal. The pieces of the puzzle are coming together."

"Good to hear. Let's have that beer soon."

"I'll call you later."

Everyone in the room was looking at me, waiting for the news. "The guy in the Chrysler is Sergeant Nicolas Bruno of the WPPD."

"We'll add him to the list," Seth said.

Linda asked, "Which one do we try to flip?"

"I don't know," Seth said, "They're all pretty long in the tooth. When we have their records, maybe we'll find a vulnerability."

"I assume they'll know that we specifically asked about them?" I said. "I'm sure they will, and that should stir them up. Maybe they'll panic and make some mistakes," Seth offered, "but it could also make them dangerous."

"I'll keep digging," I said as the meeting broke up. As I was riding the elevator down, my stomach was growling, and I realized I had nothing to eat yet today. I wandered over to Sal's Pizza for a slice, and he recognized me as I walked in.

"Dan!" he exclaimed, "I'm sorry to hear about the Jordan kid. How's the investigation going?"

"It's going. It will be mostly up to the lawyers now."

I ordered a slice and a Coke, which he would not let me pay for. While I was eating, he came and sat across from me and told me about a cop coming in a few weeks ago, inquiring if anyone had been in asking about what we saw. "I didn't mention your name, but I told him about speaking with Attorney Bodner."

"What did he look like?"

The description he gave me sounded like Detective Kidd. I kept that to myself and thanked him for the information. When I returned to my car, I called Hannah just to check on her and hear her voice.

"Hi, Dad."

"Hi, Han, how's everything?"

"All good. This is our last week of classes before finals. I'll be studying and taking tests for the next few weeks."

"Is Kristine with you all day?"

"Pretty much. I mean, she doesn't come into the classroom with me, but she's right by the door when I get out. I like her."

"Good to hear. I'd love to see you, but I'm still afraid of being followed and leading them to you."

"I understand, Dad. How much longer will it be?"

"There's no way to know. I hope not much longer."

"Okay. I miss you."

"Miss you, too. Bye, Han."

I returned to the marina to prepare for my night watchman's arrival. While driving, there was no indication of a tail, and I smiled while wondering if they had followed the produce truck around yet. I set out some towels and a sleeping bag for Dave, then cracked open a beer and sat in the cockpit, watching the activity at the marina.

At 6:00 sharp, my phone rang. It was Dave announcing his arrival. I walked to the gate, let him in, and handed him a keycard. After dropping his stuff on the boat, we strolled down the dock to the office to show him where the heads and showers were located, also accessed by the key card. We then wandered up to the diner and discussed my security concerns over dinner. I found out he was also ex-military, having served on a destroyer in the Navy. He explained that he had done plenty of dock security over a twenty-year enlistment.

When he ordered coffee after dinner, I assumed he planned to stay awake all night, which I was happy about. When we returned to the boat, I showed him where the coffee pot was stowed and told him to help himself to anything on the boat. While he was unpacking, Mia called.

"I'm at the airport, Dan. We board in an hour."

"I'm going to miss you, sweetheart. Thanks for last night."

"I loved it, too. And this morning!"

I laughed, "I checked out the link you sent me for the rental house. The ocean views look amazing; you and Judy will have a wonderful time."

"I think so too. You'll be careful while I'm gone, won't you?"

"I will, don't worry. We'll do a sailing trip when you return."

"That sounds wonderful! I love you."

"I love you too. Have fun!"

With that, she ended the call. We could have gone on forever, not wanting the call to end. I sat momentarily, imagining her at the airport, picturing her face, and recalling her scent. I knew I was hopelessly in love.

Dave and I sat in the cockpit for a while longer chatting, and I answered his questions about the case, explaining the racist group of the WPPD. Eventually, I said good night and went down to sleep with the comfort of knowing I had an armed military man on guard overnight.

CHAPTER 20

Sean O'Riley

Using the tracking device, Detective Kidd located Burnett's Grand Cherokee parked in downtown White Plains near Tibbets Park. He was able to park his Ford Explorer a few spots behind it. An hour or so later, when he saw a man approach the vehicle, he started taking pictures with his phone. This was the first time they had seen Burnett or knew what he looked like. He was taller and thinner than he had imagined. He texted the pictures to everyone else, then followed him all the way to the City Island bridge. Other than taking his picture, he learned nothing new about Burnett.

Over the next week, either O'Riley or Kidd tracked Burnett multiple times. One afternoon, Captain Owens called Detective Kidd and told him that heavy meetings were happening at the station involving the DA, Chief Allen, and Captain Johnson. Owens had been included in one meeting, which focused on whether the DA would proceed with murder charges. Kidd immediately called O'Riley and informed him of the meetings, then said, "Here's some more bad news: The attorney just requested files for every group member. He's getting inside information somewhere."

"Do we have a snitch in the group?" O'Riley asked.

"I have no idea, but this guy has to be stopped. I'm going to call a meeting ASAP and see what everyone wants to do about it."

"Good. Let me tell you about what that fuck did to me today."

"Okay, I'm listening."

"While I was following him, he and another guy ambushed me on a main road, and one of them held a gun to my head. Right in the middle of the road."

"So he knows we've been following him?"

"I guess so. He knew my name and that I had been fired."

The next morning, still using the tracking app, Kidd located Burnett's vehicle at the marina and headed that way to resume the tail when he left the island. He pulled into a golf course parking lot to wait, just on the Pelham side of the bridge. With the app open on his phone, he watched the icon move over the map to multiple places on City Island, stopping every thousand feet for several minutes before moving on. It took an hour for the icon to reach the far end of the island and another hour for it to return. He was trying to imagine what Burnett could possibly be doing. Finally, after waiting two hours, he needed to pee and used the restroom at the golf course. When he returned to his car and settled his overstuffed body behind the wheel, he reopened the app and saw the icon on the mainland, heading into Pelham. With his phone in a dashboard mount, he followed the icon on the map. He saw it had stopped near the town center and drove closer, looking for the Cherokee.

He was now in a restaurant parking lot and still could not spot Burnett's car, even though it appeared he was right next to the icon. With the phone in his hand, he walked around the parking lot, trying to pinpoint the location. It led him to a mid-size box truck parked alongside him with a Hunts Point Produce sign painted on the side. Baffled, he returned to his car, trying to figure out what was happening. A few minutes later, when the produce truck pulled out of the lot, along with the icon, he realized he'd been duped. Burnett had discovered the device and placed it on a delivery truck, wasting his entire morning.

While Kidd's morning was wasted, Sean O'Riley had better luck. While staking out the ex-wife's house in New Rochelle, he witnessed two young ladies leave in a Honda CRV and followed them to Iona University near the center of town. He watched as they parked and entered a classroom building together.

They were both attractive girls with athletic bodies and sandy blonde hair. The one with long hair was taller and carried a backpack. A few minutes later, the short-haired girl exited the building and sat in her car, only to return an hour later and escort the other girl out.

O'Riley followed them around the campus for the next few hours and saw this pattern repeated. If one was just a driver, why would she go in and out with the other? Neither of them appeared disabled in any way. After weighing the possibilities, the only explanation he could come up with was that the taller girl was Burnett's daughter, and the short-haired girl was a bodyguard, which meant they were aware of a present danger. O'Riley called Kidd and told him the details of what he had witnessed and what he had concluded. Kidd agreed that could be the only explanation.

"We'll share that information at the meeting tomorrow and see what everyone wants to do with it. By the way, the meeting is at noon at the Roadhouse."

"Good. See you there."

The Roadhouse Bar and Grill meeting had the largest attendance O'Riley could remember. In addition to himself and Detective Kidd, Captains Johnson and Owens, retired Captain Salerno, Sergeant Bruno, and the rookie Mick McGhee were there. Two members of the Proud Boys, who provided the awards and contributed financially to the group, were also in attendance. The last time they had met was when O'Riley was awarded four opening-day box seats at Yankee Stadium for putting Jerome Jordan in the hospital.

As usual, they gathered in a private, dark-paneled, windowless back room with pitchers of beer on the table. Once everyone was seated and the doors were closed, Captain Owens started the meeting by introducing the members of the Proud Boys along with Officer McGhee. Everyone else was well acquainted with one another.

Owens then said, "It sounds like this incident with the Jordan kid has brought a new level of focus on us. His attorney and investigator seem to have penetrated our secrecy and know who every one of us is. The question before us today is: what do we do about it."

After scratching his beard, Nick Bruno said, "We need to take them out."

"Are we really ready to start murdering people?" Captain Johnson asked.

"I think murdering someone will just increase the heat on us. We'll all go down for that," said Captain Owens.

"Well, we need to get them to drop the case somehow. Any ideas?" Bruno asked.

"Sean, tell everyone what you learned yesterday," Kidd said.

"I found out that Burnett has a daughter that attends Iona. I also believe she always has a bodyguard with her, another young woman."

"So they know they're in danger?" the rookie McGhee asked.

"It appears they do. I've seen a bodyguard with attorney Bodner whenever he comes and goes from the office." Kidd said. "Here's another tidbit: Burnett found our tracking device on his car. We can no longer track him."

"Can we track his phone?" Owens asked.

"We tried that already. He keeps his phone off and just turns it on occasionally to make a call. There's never time for triangulation," Kidd said.

"How about we kidnap the daughter and make them drop the case before releasing her?" Bruno suggested.

There was a pause while everyone contemplated that idea. Then Owens said, "That will require two people, one to deal with the bodyguard and another to snatch the girl."

"One of them should be you, O'Riley, since you're the cause of this mess," Captain Johnson said.

"Fine with me, Captain."

"If we do that, anyone who comes in contact with her will need to be masked; otherwise, she'll be able to identify us, and we'll have to kill her," Owens added.

"Let me surveil the daughter tomorrow and see if that's doable," Bruno offered.

"If you can figure out a way to do it, we can stash her at my lake house in Connecticut," Owens offered.

"It sounds like we have the beginnings of a plan," Captain Johnson said. "Nick, let us know what you come up with tomorrow."

After Bruno nodded, Owens said, "Okay, let's have lunch and get out of here."

Sergeant Nicolas Bruno drove his Toyota pickup to New Rochelle the following morning to observe the two girls. Once he had scoped out the house and confirmed their CRV was in the driveway, he parked on the main road and waited for them to drive by. He killed the time by playing video games on his phone. They exited the street two hours later and drove past him toward town. There was no need to follow too closely—he knew where they were going. When they reached the Iona campus, he watched as they parked and went inside the building. A few minutes later, the short-haired girl came out and sat in her car.

Then, an hour later, she went back in, and they both walked out together, just as O'Riley had described. With the same pattern repeating for the next few hours, Bruno felt he had a pretty good assessment of what they were dealing with. On the way home, he called Captain Owens and filled him in.

"Okay. Let's meet at my house tonight and come up with a plan. How about 7:00?

"Good. I'll inform Kidd and O'Riley," Bruno said.

That evening, Captain Owens, Kidd, Bruno, and O'Riley gathered on the back porch of Owens' house. Bruno confirmed what O'Riley had observed the previous day, then said, "If we try to kidnap her at the house, we won't know what we're walking into. It could be a mess that ends up in a shoot-out."

"If we do it at the school, we at least know what we're up against. We should be able to defeat the female bodyguard easily enough," O'Riley said.

"I agree. Snatching her from the bodyguard at school is the cleanest way to do it," Bruno concluded.

When they all nodded in agreement, Owens said, "Okay, We'll need two people, and as Captain Johnson said, one should be you, Sean."

"I'll go with him," Kidd said.

"Great. That's it, guys. Let's not fuck it up!" Owens exclaimed.

CHAPTER 21

Dan Burnett

was woken in the morning by the aroma of coffee brewing. I opened the door to my bunk room to find Dave sitting in the salon reading something on his phone.

"Good morning," I said. "Thanks for making coffee."

"This is the second pot. I made the first around two a.m."

"You're welcome to sleep here all day if you want."

"I may take you up on that one of these days, but today, I think I'll go home. What time do you want me this evening?"

"Just be here by dark. I'm not yet sure when I'll be back."

By the time I had showered and dressed, he was gone. While sipping coffee, I made notes in the case book of yesterday's events. While thinking about Seth's goal of getting someone to flip, I thought about calling Officer Sanchez. Now that I know more about what questions to ask, maybe I can get more information from him. Luckily, I was put through without identifying myself when I called the station.

"This is Sanchez."

"Hello, Officer. We spoke a few weeks ago on the phone in the evening," I said, not wanting to state my name on a potentially recorded line.

"Yes, I remember. Can I call you right back?"

"Sure, I'll wait for your call."

A few minutes later, he called from a different number. "Dan Burnett, I presume?"

"Yes, Thanks for the callback. We've become aware of a group of cops who hang out with Sean O'Riley. Do you know who his friends are?"

After a pause, he said, "I always saw him with Sergeant Bruno and Detective Kidd. There is also a rookie patrolman named McGhee, but since O'Riley was fired, I haven't seen them together."

"Do you have a first name for McGhee?"

"Mick. Mick McGhee."

"Thanks, Officer. Can you keep this between us?"

"For sure, you didn't get that name from me."

"Agreed," I said before ending the call.

I thought for a few moments, wondering how to identify McGhee. A phone call would not serve my purpose. I could walk into the police station and ask to look at the picture book again, but by now, they might be on the lookout for me. I called Frosty once again for motor vehicle records.

"Detective Frost."

"Hi, Matt. It's Dan again. How about that beer this afternoon?"

"Sure. Murph's?"

"Yeah, while I've got you, can you look up another registration for me?"

"Jesus, Dan. Maybe you need your own DMV terminal."

"If only it were legal!" I exclaimed.

"Okay, Give it to me."

"Mick McGhee. M, C, capital G, H, E, E. He's a rookie cop at WPPD."

"I'll call you back."

"Thanks, buddy."

While waiting on Frosty, I called Seth's office with this new name to see how he wanted to proceed. Paula put me right through.

"Good morning, Dan. What's up?"

"I just got the name of a rookie cop who's chummy with O'Riley and the others. Do you want to add him to your list of record requests?"

"Hmm, do you think you could speak with him first? Maybe he's the one we try to flip."

"It's worth a try. I should have his DMV records shortly."

"Good. See what you can do. If you strike out, I'll add him to the list."

"Okay, I'll keep you posted."

"Bye, Dan."

Two minutes later, Frosty called, "Here's what I've got. Michael McGhee drives a black 2018 Camaro, tag number EYG-285. His address is 442 Glendale Road, White Plains."

"Thank you. 5:15 at Murph's?"

"I'll be there."

With that information, I turned off my phone and left for White Plains.

Because it was midday, I thought I'd look for his car first behind the station. Keeping an eye on the mirror the whole way, I never saw a tail. When I drove past the police parking lot, I slowed and looked for the Camaro. Seeing no signs of it, I parked, called the station using the burner phone, and asked for Patrolman McGhee. I was told he was on the night shift this week and wouldn't be in until 5:00. Not wanting to wait around all day, I chose to take a ride by his home address. After turning my phone back on, I punched the address into Google Maps and saw Glendale Road was off Route 22, only a few minutes away. When I arrived, the Camaro was in the driveway, and I saw a man with curly red hair, relatively small in stature, playing catch with a young boy in the side yard. I stopped in front of the house, exited my Jeep, and stood leaning against the rear hatch. It wasn't long before he sent the boy into the house and approached me. As he got closer, I recognized him from the Roadhouse photos.

"Can I help you?" he said.

"Maybe I can help you," I replied.

"How so?"

"I'm a private investigator employed by the attorney representing the Jordan family," I said, noticing the name Jordan got his attention.

"I'll ask again. How can I help you?"

"It has come to our attention that you were friendly with Officer O'Riley, Detective Kidd, and Sergeant Bruno."

"Yes, I know them; we're all cops here in town."

He started to fidget and looked nervous. I continued, "What do you know about white supremacist groups?"

His face began to turn red, causing his freckles to blend together. "Nothing. I will ask you to leave before I call for backup."

"Before you do that, I have a proposition for you."

"I'm listening."

"We have reliable information that there is a white supremacist group within the WPPD. It's been going on for many years and includes the names I just mentioned, Captain Owens, and others. We also know that you're chummy with this group."

"Where did you hear that?"

"That's not important. I can tell you that Attorney Bodner has issued a subpoena for all of them. He plans to issue one for you, too, but I thought a young family man like you, with his whole life ahead of him, might not want to go down with the rest of them. Are you aware of the federal penalties for hate crimes?"

After a few moments of silence, with him looking me in the eyes, he said, "What are you proposing?"

"If you make a sworn statement implicating the cops in the group, Attorney Bodner will exclude you from the civil suit."

"How long do I have to think about this?"

"Until noon tomorrow," I replied, handing him a card with the burner phone number.

He nodded, then turned and walked into his house without saying a word.

While on my way to the Bronx to meet Frosty, I called Seth, told him about my conversation, and suggested he keep some time open tomorrow afternoon.

I walked into Murph's a few minutes before 5:00 and chatted with a few cops I had worked with at the 49th Precinct. When Murph saw me at the bar, he opened a Heineken and set it before me.

"How's it going, Dan? It's been a while."

"All good, Murph. Frosty should be by in a while."

"Happy to hear you guys have remained friends."

"Yeah, I'm happy about that, too."

A few minutes later, Matt entered, and we moved to a booth across from the bar. Within moments, Murph carried over a Guinness and said, "How you been, Frosty?"

"I'm fine, Murph. How's business?"

"Same old, same old," he replied, returning behind the bar.

"So, tell me what all these DMV requests are about," Frosty said.

"This might be hard to believe, but there's a group of white supremacist cops in White Plains."

"White Plains? That's an affluent, educated slice of suburbia in a very blue county—a long way from Mississippi."

"That's what I thought, too. It seems they've come out of the woodwork over the last several years."

"Yeah, and bolder than ever," Matt added.

"The cops in this group range from rookies all the way up to Captains."

"It sounds like this has been going on for a while?"

"We have evidence going back nearly a decade."

"What does Bodner plan to do with this?"

"We're hoping to flip one, cut him a deal, and have him testify. Cops are going down on this—it will rock the country."

"I'm amazed at the high-profile cases you've been working on since you retired," Matt said.

"Me too. I thought I'd be taking pictures of cheating spouses," I laughed.

We remained in the booth for another round while he told me about the cases he was working and I updated him on the security details at Sheila's and the marina. When Frosty finished his second beer, he went home for dinner with his family while I stayed behind for some fish and chips.

Upon returning to Privateer, I saw that Dave was already there, walking the docks, looking for anything unusual. I kept him company in the cockpit for a while before going below for the night.

When I awoke, I saw an email from Mia had come in overnight. After doing some quick math, I realized it was the afternoon in Portugal. In her email, she told me how much she was enjoying Lisbon and the hotel they were staying at. She said they had both scheduled massages that afternoon and told me how much she had already missed me. I replied that I missed her and that maybe we could figure out a time to chat on the phone. After hitting send, I went to the galley and poured myself a coffee.

Once I had dressed for the day, Dave took off after confirming he'd return before dark. With nothing to do except wait for Mick McGhee to call, I spent the morning cleaning the inside of the boat and doing laundry at the machines by the office. At 11:00, McGhee called.

"You can take your offer and stick it up your ass! Cops don't talk about cops." He hung up before I could respond.

I sat in the cockpit with the burner phone in my hand, wondering what was going through his head. I assumed he had told the other cops about my offer, and they convinced him to stay silent. I called Seth and told him about the call.

"So it's safe to say that the entire group knows how close we are to taking them down. This is a dangerous time for us, Dan. Make sure the security detail with your daughter and ex-wife is on full alert, and you need to be on your toes. They're not going to take this lying down."

"You're right, Seth. I'm going to back up the detail on them myself."

"That's a good idea. I'll inform everyone at the office of the situation.

Check-in with us every few hours so we know you're okay."

"Will do."

My next call was to Frank Wright. I explained the reason for the heightened alert and told him I was on my way to provide backup.

"I'll be leaving soon to pick up Sheila from work. Hannah and Kristine are still here but will be leaving in an hour for Iona," he said.

"I'll be there well before that."

CHAPTER 22

Before leaving the marina, I rechecked my car for another tracking device. Not finding one, I headed for New Rochelle. Hannah and Kristine were sitting in the kitchen, awaiting my arrival. I explained that I was there just in an abundance of caution and had complete confidence in Kristine. After confirming that she and I had each other's cell numbers in our phones, they left for Iona in her Honda CRV. I followed, staying as far behind them as I dared, looking for anyone tailing them. I had seen nothing when we arrived on campus.

Kristine walked with Hannah into the building, returned to the parking lot, and sat with me in the car. After chatting for a few minutes, I called Ron Horton, the head of campus security, and told him about our presence. Kristine filled me in on Hannah's schedule for the day. After this class, she had an hour off, followed by another class in a different building. Then, she was done for the day and would return home. I asked her if Hannah resented having a shadow, and she explained they had become friends and enjoyed each other's company.

An hour later, Kristine went into the building and escorted Hannah out. The two of them walked to the cafeteria for lunch, came out a half-hour later, and then Hannah rode with Kristine to the other side of the campus, with me following. Once again, they entered a building together. I had parked on the far side of the lot, and while they were inside, I noticed a dark gray Toyota pick-up cruise through the lot, slow to observe Kristine's car, then exit, only to park in the lot across the street, the driver remaining in the vehicle. I took a picture of the vehicle and then texted Kristine, telling her not to come to my car when she exited.

I saw her check her phone as she exited the building before going to her car. The Toyota stayed put, and I observed a glint of light reflect off what I assumed were binoculars from the driver's side. I called Kristine and filled her in on what I had witnessed, and told her I would follow them back to the house with some space between us.

Kristine entered the building an hour later, escorted Hannah to her car, and drove off. The Toyota pick-up followed with one car between them. About halfway to Sheila's, the Toyota turned right onto a side street while I kept my distance behind Kristine. A few blocks later, the Toyota reappeared, this time two cars behind them. I assumed he knew where they were heading and made a quick around-the-block detour to disguise the tail or see if anyone was following him. Whatever his intention, it was a fruitless attempt.

I remained well behind them both, and when Kristine and Hannah turned down the cul-de-sac street to the house, the Toyota continued with me several cars back. While I followed, I called Kristine again to let her know what I was doing and told her I'd keep her posted.

On the outskirts of New Rochelle, the Toyota entered a Home Depot parking lot. Keeping my distance, I followed and watched the driver park and enter the store. Once he had been in the store for a minute, I parked in the row in front of him, placed a tracking device under his right front wheel well, and drove to the other side of the lot.

I checked to ensure my phone was properly linked to the device, then returned to Sheila's.

While sitting in the driveway, I called Seth's office, told Paula I was just checking in, and gave her a brief report of what I had been doing all day. I then called Frosty with another request for DMV information, this time for the Toyota pickup.

"No problem, Dan. Is everyone safe today?"

"So far. I discovered the Toyota following Hannah."

"I'll get on it right now. Do you want to hold?"

"Sure."

A minute later, he came back on the line. "That truck is also registered to Nicolas Bruno, the same as the Chrysler."

"Thanks, I appreciate it."

Before going into the house, I thought I would call Alejandro Perez, a detective with the New Rochelle Police Department. He was Hannah's soccer coach for many years while growing up, and I helped solve a case of his last year. Scanning through my contacts, I found his cell number and made the call.

"Hey, Dan, it's been a while. How are you?"

"Pretty good, Alejandro. I need to ask you for a favor."

"Sure, anything."

I told him about working on the Jordan case, the security at the house, and Hannah being followed today. I asked if he could send a patrol car by the house overnight and keep an eye out for anything suspicious.

"Sure, I'll add the address to the patrol list. What are we looking for?"

"I'll be sitting in the driveway overnight in a Grand Cherokee. We have identified the vehicles that have been following us. Can you put out a BOLO on them?"

"Sure, give me the list."

I repeated the description of the vehicles with the plate numbers of all the cars owned by the members of the Supremacist group, which totaled six cars.

"Do you want us to pull them over and run their info?"

"Only if they're near the house. I should also tell you they are White Plains cops."

"Bad cops?"

"We think so. One of them killed the Jordan kid."

"Okay, Dan. I'll notify you if we see any of those vehicles near the house."

"Thanks, Alejandro. I owe you one."

"I'm not keeping score, Dan," he said before ending the call.

When I entered Sheila's house, they were drinking coffee in the kitchen.

After joining them at the table, Hannah poured me a cup and said, "Is everything all right, Dad?"

"Yes, Han. I was just on the phone with Alejandro Perez. He will send a patrol car by from time to time this evening and also keep an eye out for the pickup truck that was following you. I'm going to sit in my car overnight in the driveway."

Frank said, "Kristine told us about the truck—do you know who was driving?"

"I ran the plate; it's registered to a White Plains cop. I assume he was driving."

"This is scary, Dan," Sheila said.

"Well, you'll have three guards here tonight, and the police will keep a lookout. I'm sure we'll be fine."

"If you say so," she said. "Will you be having dinner with us?"

"Only if you have enough to go around," I replied.

"We're having spaghetti and meatballs—there's plenty."

"Thank you. I love your meatballs."

After dinner, while Hannah and Sheila were cleaning up, Frank, Kristine, and I discussed a strategy for the evening. Knowing it would be challenging to stay awake all night, we agreed on set times for each of us to sleep, two hours at a time. The plan provided for two of us to be awake at all times. At 9:00, I went out to the car with a thermos of coffee and an old coat I found in the garage that I used to wear when shoveling snow. I could always start the car and run the heat, but I hoped I wouldn't need to if I used the coat as a blanket. I opened the tracker app on my phone and saw that the Toyota pickup was parked in a residential neighborhood in Tarrytown—most likely Bruno's house. All remained quiet in the neighborhood until I got a call from Alejandro around three a.m. Their patrol car had stopped the black Explorer two blocks from the house with two guys in it. The driver flashed a badge, but they still asked for IDs before letting them continue on. The names were William Kidd and Sean O'Riley.

When the sun came up around 7:00, I texted Frank that I was leaving and also about Alejandro's call before driving to the marina. Dave was just on his way out when I arrived, and he told me he had a quiet night. I then went below and slept until noon.

When I awoke, a text from Seth was waiting for me. They had received the requested records from the police department, had been reviewing them all morning, and wanted to know if I could come in that afternoon. I texted back that I'd be there at 2:00. After showering and changing clothes, I grabbed a bacon and egg sandwich at the diner before heading to White Plains, seeing no signs of a tail on my way there.

CHAPTER 23

Seth, Linda, and Paula were in the conference room when I arrived. After Paula brought me a coffee, Seth updated us on the recently obtained records.

"Kidd, Bruno, and Owens all have disciplinary action in their records pertaining to violence, all occurring with non-white victims. Owens' one incident was ten years ago before he was made Captain. Kidd and Bruno were both suspended for an incident in 2016 for discharging their firearms in a residential apartment while executing a search warrant. No weapons were found in the apartment. Bruno was suspended again in 2019 after beating a young Hispanic man during a traffic stop," Seth concluded. He had been reading from a summary and handed me a copy.

"So that's more evidence that a group exists," I said.

"It certainly is. I think we have enough evidence of hate crimes to bring to the United States Attorney for the Southern District of New York," he added.

"Are you suggesting that we let them take over our case?" Linda asked. "Not at all. There's no guarantee they will pursue the case or how long it might take. Our job is to have the Jordan family financially compensated for the loss of their son. A federal criminal case will not do that, but if they bring charges, it will certainly bolster our case," Seth said.

I then filled them in on my experience yesterday, with Hannah being followed by Sergeant Bruno and me spending the night in the driveway. I also informed them of Kidd and O'Riley being stopped in the neighborhood at three a.m.

"Is that stop on the record?" Seth asked. "Yes, with the New Rochelle P.D."

"That's great. I'll request a copy. I'd love to hear an explanation of why the two of them were there at three a.m."

I debated telling them about the tracking device I had placed on Bruno's pickup but chose against it because tracking someone without a warrant was illegal.

"Dan, right now, I want you to protect yourself and your family. We have plenty to work with for the time being. If something comes up we need your expertise for, we'll let you know," Seth concluded.

"Thanks, Seth. Do you plan to make another public announcement?"

"Not quite yet. I'd like to hear how the U.S. Attorney reacts first."

With that, the meeting adjourned, and I left the office and headed for New Rochelle. While driving, I called Kristine to see where they were, but the call went to voice mail. I left a message for her to return my call and continued south. Frank called ten minutes later and said Kristine had missed her check-in call.

"When was she supposed to check in?" I asked.

"At 3:00. They should have been on their way back to the house by then."

"Okay, I'm heading for Iona. Let me know as soon as you hear from her."

"Will do, Dan. This is not like her; she always makes the call."

"I get the picture. Let's hope for the best."

When I arrived on campus, there were patrol cars everywhere. When I reached the driveway to Hannah's dorm, barricades blocked the entrance, and a cop stopped all traffic. I got out of the car and asked him what was going on, and he told me there had been a shooting. When I told him my daughter was in there and asked if he'd let me through, he said no one was allowed in.

I called Alejandro's cell, and he asked me to hold a moment while I heard him giving orders in the background.

A few moments later, he said, "There has been a shooting in an Iona parking lot. It might be your daughter's bodyguard. We haven't located Hannah yet."

My heart sank, and I felt like throwing up. My mind was racing as I tried to figure out what to do. Remembering Alejandro was still on the line, I asked him where he was. When he said he was in the parking lot, I told him I was on campus and asked if he would tell his patrol officer to allow me through. He said he would call him on the radio. I returned to my car with my mind still racing and waited for a signal from the officer. A minute later, he waived me through.

I parked in the lot, trying to leave room for the first responders to work. As I approached the scene, I saw the paramedics loading a gurney into the ambulance, and then Alejandro appeared beside me.

"We checked the ID of the female in the ambulance—her name is Kristine Wallace. Is that Hannah's bodyguard?"

"It is. Is she alive?"

"She is, but has a bullet wound to the neck. It looks like she was driving the car, and someone shot her through the driver's side window. There's a lot of blood, but the paramedics said they were hopeful. The last time Hannah was seen was while getting in the car."

I took a moment to regulate my breathing, hoping to get my heart rate under control. With minimal success, I said, "How about her things—her backpack?"

"Her backpack was in the car, and her cell phone was in the backpack."

"Shit. I was hoping I could use that to locate her."

"I know. I hoped so, too. We're asking everyone if they saw anything; so far, nothing."

"Have you checked with campus security? They have some surveillance cameras."

"Mr. Horton is going through the recordings now. We'll see what he finds."

When Alejandro was called back to Kristine's CRV, I called Frank Wright to share what I knew.

"Kristine was shot in the neck through the side window of her car. She's lost some blood, but the paramedics are optimistic. She should be at the hospital any minute now."

"How about Hannah?"

"So far, There's no sign of her. I think she was abducted because her backpack and cell phone were found in Kristine's car."

"What would you like me to do?"

"Stay with Sheila. I know I should be the one to tell her, but I don't want to do it on the phone, and I know she won't take it well. Can you tell her?"

"I'll take care of it, Dan. Keep me posted."

"I will. Thanks."

Alejandro approached and asked me to check in with Ron Horton. When I did, he said, "I've seen no signs of Hannah or an abduction. Are there any specific vehicles you want us to be looking for?"

I listed each vehicle we knew was owned by the supremacist cops but could only remember the HUNTER license plate without my casebook handy. I told him I could confirm the plates of any vehicles matching the descriptions.

"Okay. Now that I know what to look for, I'll get back to you."

"Thanks, Ron."

By now, my heart rate and breathing had come down enough for me to function, but were still nowhere near normal. I was having an anxiety attack and felt the need to do something. After a few deep breaths, I called Seth and let him know what had transpired.

After Paula put me through, I said, "Hannah's bodyguard has been shot, and Hannah is missing."

"Fuck! What can I do, Dan?"

"I don't know. I was hoping sharing this would calm me down."

"Do you want me to come down there?"

I paused a moment and said, "No. If she's been kidnapped, maybe they'll call your office."

"Is the bodyguard alive?"

"So far. The paramedics are hopeful."

"I'm so sorry to hear about this. I'll let you know if we get a call. You have my cell number, right?"

"I do."

My anxiety had turned to anger, mainly anger at myself for involving my family. I wished I could call Mia for some emotional support, but it was nearly midnight where she was. I headed to Sheila's, hoping we might comfort each other. Or maybe I just needed to face the medicine.

While driving, Ron Horton called to inform me that none of the vehicles I had listed were seen in the surveillance video from that day. I thanked him for the effort, and he said he would keep looking.

When I arrived at the house, Frank greeted me in the driveway. "She's not taking it well, Dan."

"I can't imagine she is. Maybe she can vent on me."

Once inside, I found Sheila crying at the kitchen table. When I approached her and put a hand on her shoulder, she rose and started punching me in the chest. Over and over, she pounded my chest with her face twisted in anger until she was exhausted and her legs would no longer support her. I hugged her to prevent her from collapsing on the floor, and she sobbed while her arms were pinned to my chest. I had been crying, too, and we remained in the embrace, comforting each other for quite a while.

Eventually, we sat at the table, wiping our faces with napkins while she continued to sob, her whole body shuddering from time to time. Frank entered the kitchen with a report from the hospital that Kristine was in stable condition after surgery. Sheila and I both expressed our joy at that news, but it wasn't long before we returned to grieving. Within a few more minutes, I realized that crying it out with her had relieved some anxiety, and I could again focus on the task at hand.

I called Frosty and Jim and told them the situation, and they both said they would be here within an hour. Just the thought of my former and current partner's support made me feel hopeful. When I told Sheila they were coming, it also seemed to lift her spirits.

When Frosty arrived, he hugged Sheila, comforting her. Once Jim arrived, we gathered at the table, and I reviewed everything I knew with them, including the names, addresses, and vehicle information of the cops involved. After some brainstorming, we concluded that until there was a demand from the kidnappers, the only thing we could do was stake out the cop's houses and follow their vehicles if they left.

Sheila offered to make sandwiches, but none of us had an appetite. She turned on the news to see how they were covering the shooting at Iona, and we saw Alejandro being interviewed, telling the reporter that they had no new information at this time. He went on to say that Iona had always been a peaceful campus and that there was no explanation for the shooting. He made no mention of Hannah's kidnapping. By the time the news concluded, it was becoming dark outside.

We left Frank at the house to guard Sheila, and Jim, Frosty, and I headed out to the cops' known addresses. We determined that I would scope out O'Riley and McGhee because they both lived in White Plains, not far from each other. Jim would stake out Bruno in Tarrytown, and Frosty would check on Kidd in Hartsdale and Owens in Scarsdale. Since we didn't yet have a street address for Owens, Frosty could obtain it using his active police credentials.

I cruised by O'Riley's Greenridge Road address first and saw no car in the driveway or any lights on in the house. Next, I went past McGhee's house and saw the Camaro in the driveway, with the house well-lit.

Because both of these cops knew what my Grand Cherokee looked like, I tried my best not to attract attention. I parked down the street from McGhee's house, where I could see if his car moved. Remembering I could track Bruno's pickup, I checked the location on my phone, saw it was at his house in Tarrytown, and called Jim to share that information. He had not yet arrived.

Later that evening, I saw McGhee's house lights go out, with the car still in the driveway. After another half-hour, I drove past O'Riley's house and saw the Mustang in the driveway, with a few lights on within the house. I parked where I could keep an eye on the house and called Frosty. He reported that he saw Kidd's Explorer enter the garage a half hour ago and thought he could see him moving around in the house. He also noted that Owens' house had a three-car garage and that someone was home but saw no one coming or going.

When I touched base with Jim again, he confirmed the pickup was in the driveway, and there was no sign of the Chrysler. However, it could be in the garage. We called each other every hour or so, mainly to keep one another awake. When the lights went out in O'Riley's house, I walked to his car and placed a tracking device under the right rear wheel well. I could now track two of their vehicles.

A little after six a.m., as the eastern sky began to lighten, Frosty reported that the Ram pickup had pulled out of the garage, and he was following it. A while later, he called in and said the pickup was heading north on Route 684.

Shortly before 7:00, he called again and said he would have to give up the tail because his shift started in one hour at Precinct 49. I thanked him for his overnight help and wondered how he planned to stay awake for the rest of the day.

I called Jim and told him about Frosty abandoning his tail of Owens on 684. Jim said he would stay in Tarrytown until 8:00, when he planned to go home for some sleep. A few minutes later, he called back and said the Chrysler had just pulled into the driveway—it had been gone all night. When I thanked him for the help, he told me he'd be available again that afternoon.

I planned to watch O'Riley until he moved or I could no longer stay awake.

A while later, I checked in with Frank to see how the night went and if he had received any news about Kristine.

"There's nothing new on Kristine, but Sheila had a rough night without sleep. She called her school for a substitute and took a pill around sunup. I believe she's asleep at the moment."

"Good. I plan to go to my boat for some sleep unless I'm needed there."

"No, we'll be fine. I'll call you if that changes."

"Thanks, Frank. We're fortunate to have you."

"Bye, Dan."

When I arrived at the boat, Dave had left a note reporting another quiet night at the marina and that he would return before dark. I washed my face, hit the bunk, and had a fitful sleep, worried for Hannah.

CHAPTER 24

My ringtone jarred me out of a deep dream. It took me a few moments to remember where I was, and I noticed it was only a few minutes after 10:00.

"Hello."

"Dan, it's Seth. Did I wake you?"

"Yeah. I pulled an all-nighter watching O'Riley's house."

"Sorry about that. How's your ex taking it?"

"Not good. She was up all night."

"I'm calling to tell you that we just heard from the kidnappers. They said your daughter is fine and will be released if we drop our investigation."

"What did you say?"

"I told them to call back at noon and to have her speak with her father.

Can you be here by then?"

"Absolutely! I'll be there soon."

"Good, Dan. We're all keeping our fingers crossed."

"Thanks, Seth."

I was now wide awake but needed a shower and some coffee. When that was accomplished, I called Frank. "Is Sheila awake?"

"Yes, we're having coffee in the kitchen."

"Put her on, please."

"Hello, Dan?"

"Yes, It's me. We just heard from the kidnappers; they called the attorney's office and told him Hannah was fine and would be returned safely if we dropped the case."

"Will you?"

"Of course. We'll do whatever they ask for her safe return. I hope to speak with Hannah when they call back at noon."

"You let me know the minute you speak with her."

"You know I will. I'll call you then."

"Okay."

After ending the call, I left for Seth's office, arriving around 11:30. Paula rose and hugged me while Linda looked at me sympathetically. We all gathered in the conference room, where Seth relayed his discussions with the United States Attorney.

"He wants the case. I sent over the files from WPPD yesterday, along with your reports, and he's assigned a team to it already. He just called me back and said two of the cops' pictures matched images of wanted insurrectionists from January 6 at the Capitol."

"So we can tell the kidnappers we're dropping the case?"

"Yes. The FBI will investigate, and we'll let them do all the dirty work.

When those cops are charged with hate crimes, the city of White Plains will be begging us to settle."

"Good to hear, Seth. I can't wait to speak with Hannah."

"We should hear from them any minute now."

Noon came and went, and when 12:10 came and went, I began pacing. At 12:15, when the call came in, Paula sent it to the conference room, and Seth put it on speaker.

"So, have you agreed to drop the case?" we heard in an electronically disguised male voice.

Seth replied, "Before we agree to anything, we want to hear Hannah speak with her father; he's right here."

A moment later, we heard, "Dad? Are you there?"

Recognizing her voice immediately, I replied, "Yes, Han, I'm here. Are you okay?"

"I'm fine, but I'm scared."

That was all she was allowed to say. The disguised male voice said, "See?

We haven't hurt her."

Seth then said, "We'll drop the suit immediately. Where can we pick her up?"

"As soon as we can confirm that you've withdrawn the lawsuit, we'll call back—maybe tomorrow," he said before ending the call.

Stunned by the abrupt response, we sat silently, dealing with our frustration. I found myself grinding my teeth.

"Can you trace that call?" I asked.

"I can tell from the odd area code that it's a burner phone. The call was too short anyway."

I went out to the outer office and called Sheila. She answered immediately. "Did you speak with her?"

"I did. She sounded fine but said she was scared."

"When are we getting her back?"

"They said as soon as they confirm that we dropped the case."

"How will they confirm that?"

"I don't know. I'll leave that to Seth."

"Ask him; I need to know."

"Okay, I'll speak to you soon."

Momentarily, I remained in the chair, completely understanding her need to know. I returned to the conference room and asked Seth how he planned to officially drop the case.

"I'll file papers this afternoon, withdrawing our civil suit," he replied. "You'll do that?"

"Certainly. I'll need to explain it to the Jordan family first, but yes, I'll do it within the hour. Linda, will you prepare the papers?"

"Already on it," she replied

"Can we keep the U.S. Attorney from making an announcement?" I asked.

"Announcements are not something they usually do, but I'll tell him about our delicate situation."

"Thanks. Sheila will be happy to hear that."

"I understand, Dan. I hope that brings her some comfort."

"I'm afraid the only thing that will bring her comfort is seeing Hannah, safe and sound, with her own eyes."

Seth just nodded with an empathetic look on his face.

While on my way to see Sheila, I called Jim and Frosty and filled them in on the last few hours' events. They were both overjoyed to hear that I had spoken with Hannah. When they asked if they were needed tonight, I told them no, but if her return did not go down tomorrow as expected, we would talk then.

When I arrived, I knocked on the front door before letting myself in. I found Sheila and Frank on the couch in front of the TV and sensed that I had interrupted something, but I thought nothing more of it as she offered me coffee while heading into the kitchen. She wanted to hear every word Hannah said in our brief conversation. After repeating her words, I explained that the lawsuit would be dropped any minute now and could be confirmed by the town clerk. I was also sure the news would spread throughout the police department like wildfire.

She then told me about Hannah's boyfriend, Ken, coming by the house and asking what he could do to help. She said he was genuinely upset and wanted to be included in any plans to rescue her. After thinking momentarily, I told her I couldn't imagine anything he could do to help without putting himself in danger.

Frank joined us a few minutes later, and we discussed how we hoped the next twenty-four hours would play out. Once I felt Sheila would be okay, I excused myself and headed to the marina for some much-needed sleep. Dave was already on the boat when I arrived and asked about Kristine. I told him what I knew before going below, and once in my bunk, I checked the tracking device app on my phone. I saw that O'Riley was on the move, heading north on Route 684, and the pickup belonging to Bruno was at his home.

As I lay in bed, I imagined what Hannah was going through and hoped she wasn't being abused. The more I thought about it, the more anxious I became. I tossed and turned, trying to sleep, but my concern for Hannah was too much to bear. I went to the galley, poured myself some bourbon, and returned to my bunk with the glass. While sipping on it, I opened the tracking app again. This time, I saw O'Riley's car stopped in Danbury, Connecticut, near Candlewood Lake. I zoomed in on the map and narrowed the location to an address on Rocky Point Road, near Bear Mountain Road. As I pondered what he might be doing there, my exhaustion overcame me, and I slept until the sunrise illuminated the overhead hatch. As I awoke, I recalled wondering about the address in Danbury and opened the tracking app again. I now saw that O'Riley had returned home, and his car was in his driveway. With the app already open, I checked on Bruno's pickup and saw it was now in Danbury at the exact location on Rocky Point Road. Bingo! That must be where they're holding Hannah!

I went to the galley and poured myself a cup of coffee from a warm pot that Dave had left behind. Then, I paced around the salon, trying to think of any reason my initial conclusion wasn't just wishful thinking. Finding nothing to dissuade me, I got dressed and headed for Danbury. Along the way, I checked in with Frank and called Jim to tell him where I was heading and why.

"Be careful up there, Dan. They know your car, and you don't want to endanger Hannah. Play this cool, buddy."

"If I can get an address, I can find out who owns the house from the tax records," I said.

"I understand. Do you want to wait until I can meet you, and then we can go in my car?"

"I'm halfway there now, Jim. I'll just do a drive-by, get the number off the mailbox, and go to City Hall."

"Okay, call me when you know something. If I don't hear from you by ten, I'm coming to look for you," Jim said.

When I exited Route 684, I headed east on Route 37 for several miles to Bear Mountain Road and again opened the app for directions. The tracking device showed Bruno's pickup was still there, so I followed the map until I reached the intersection of Rocky Point Road. I immediately saw the pickup, the only vehicle in the first driveway on the left, at a small clapboard cottage with the number "3" on the mailbox. I continued past on Bear Mountain Road without turning onto Rocky Point. While heading into town, I followed Siri's directions to the Danbury tax assessor's office, and in a few minutes, I had a copy of the file card in my hand. The owner of 3 Rocky Point was Douglas Owens.

I went into a coffee shop near City Hall for breakfast and called Jim from a booth by the window.

He answered with, "So what did you find out?"

"Douglas Owens, our police captain, owns a cottage at 3 Rocky Point Road, Danbury, Connecticut."

"No shit. Shall we go through what we know?"

"Sure, here we go: One of the white supremacist cops owns a cottage an hour away. I've tracked two of the cop's vehicles to the house, one of which is there as we speak, and Frosty witnessed another heading that way. All since her abduction. If all that doesn't add up to where Hannah is being held, I can't imagine what would."

Jim was silent momentarily, then said, "I agree, Dan. That has to be the place. What do you want to do?"

"Nothing right now. While I'm tempted to stake out the cottage, we're all good if they turn her over today as they said they would. If they don't, we devise a plan to get her out of there ASAP."

"Okay, that makes sense. I'm keeping my fingers crossed."

"Me too. I'm heading back to New-Ro now. I'll keep you posted."

CHAPTER 25

Sean O'Riley

A few minutes before noon, O'Riley and Kidd watched the two girls leave the neighborhood in the CRV and head toward Iona. Knowing their destination, they were able to follow well behind. The girls parked in a lot and went into the classroom building together, and as had been the routine, the bodyguard came out a few minutes later to wait in the car.

Parked nearby, with ski masks pulled over their heads, they planned to grab them both on their way out before reaching the car. However, it did not quite work out that way. The girls exited the building among a crowd of students. They were all laughing and cheering on their way to some event, and there was no way to snatch her from the crowd. It wasn't until they were in the car and heading out of the lot that they got their opportunity. At the stop sign, they rushed the car, one on each side with their guns along their sides. They tried to open the doors but found them locked, so O'Riley shot the driver through the window, causing them to roll into another car a few feet away and come to a stop. O'Riley reached through the broken glass and unlocked the doors while Kidd pulled the daughter out of the passenger's side door. With a firm grip, he used his sheer mass to drag her kicking and screaming into the back seat of their Explorer while O'Riley drove out the exit at a high rate of speed. The daughter kept punching and kicking until Kidd managed to handcuff and blindfold her and force a gag in her mouth. Only then could they remove the hot, itchy ski masks. Eventually, she quieted down as they drove to Owens' lake house in Danbury, Connecticut.

O'Riley and Kidd worried about getting her into the house without a neighbor seeing them as they approached the lake house. Kidd called Owens to get the lay of the land.

"There aren't any neighbors close by, but just to be safe, pull along the left side of the cottage and take her in the back door. There's a key under the mat," Owens instructed. "I'll be up to relieve you guys tonight."

They did exactly that and had no problems. Once they were in the house, O'Riley took the girl to the bathroom in case she needed to pee and closed the door. When she came out, he took her to the rear bedroom and handcuffed her to the bed with one cuff on her wrist and the other around the headboard post. After pulling his mask back down, he removed her blindfold, and she glanced around the room, getting her bearings; when he asked her name, she spit in his eye. His temper flared, and he swatted her with the back of his hand, splitting her lower lip and knocking her back onto the bed. He then left the room and closed the door behind him.

After removing the mask and wiping the spit from his face in the bathroom, he returned to the living room, where Kidd was on the phone with Owens, discussing a call to the attorney with their demands. From what he overheard, Owens was preparing to make the call.

O'Riley walked around checking out the cottage and looked to see what was in the fridge. Beer, orange juice, mayonnaise, mustard, and catsup. That was about it. Opening the cabinets, he found a box of cereal, some stale crackers, and some dishes. In the left rear corner of the cottage was a dining table with a sliding glass door that opened to a deck. Beyond that was a steep slope with a partial view of the lake below them, a quarter mile away. The furnishings were mismatched hand-me-downs, probably old pieces from Owens' house in Scarsdale.

The TV worked, however, and he and Kidd spent the rest of the afternoon watching Fox News and their continuous coverage of all the immigrants coming across the Mexican border, ruining our country.

O'Riley said, "Look at all those animals. The cameramen should be armed with machine guns instead of cameras."

"You got that right—they should mow 'em down!"

They saw Owens' Ram pickup pull into the driveway just as the sun began to set. Kidd went out the front door to greet him, then carried in a few bags of groceries.

"How do you like my summer cottage?" he asked.

"I like it," O'Riley replied. "How did the call with the attorney go?"

"I figured we should make the call in the morning. Bruno is bringing up an electronic voice modulator and a burner phone. There's no way I want the call traced or my voice recorded."

"That's smart," Kidd said. "The girl is handcuffed to the bed in the back room without a blindfold."

Owens pulled on his mask, opened the bedroom door, and told the girl, "We'll leave you like that if you remain calm and peaceful. Otherwise, we'll tie your legs and put a gag and blindfold on you. If your old man and the lawyer play it smart, you'll be home in a day or two."

The girl remained silent, staring blankly at him, not acknowledging his presence. He closed the door and returned to the kitchen to put away the groceries.

Owens said to the others, "You guys might as well take off. Bruno should be here in an hour; I think I can handle her until then."

"Okay, Captain. What time do you want us here tomorrow?" Kidd asked. "How about five or six in the afternoon? Then I can be home in time for dinner."

"See you then," Kidd said as he and O'Riley went out the door.

When the others had left, Owens went to the fridge and cracked open a beer. After a few sips, he removed a submarine sandwich from a bag and cut off a piece for the girl. After pulling on his ski mask, he brought it to her on a paper plate with a bottle of water. Again, she did not acknowledge his presence, but he left it on a chair within reach and figured if she were hungry, she would eat. Then he sat in front of the TV and ate the rest of the sandwich.

An hour later, Nick Bruno arrived. Once settled inside the cottage and masked, he checked on the girl and saw her cuffed to the bed, lying on her back, staring at the ceiling. He and Owens then discussed a sleep schedule. The plan was for one to be awake while the other slept in four-hour shifts. Owens was first to sleep, entering the bedroom around 8:00. When he came out at midnight to swap places with Bruno, he cracked the door open and peeked in at the girl. She was sound asleep while the sandwich and water remained untouched.

In the morning, after eating breakfast, Owens and Bruno set up the phone for the call. After activating the burner phone, Bruno hooked up the voice modulator, and they adjusted it so it would sound lower in pitch and somewhat distorted. Owens called Bruno's phone to test it, and they were both happy with the sound. With it still too early to call, they went out on the back deck to enjoy the lake view over the thick green trees below.

After an hour, Owens went in to check on the girl. Pulling the mask on and off was becoming a pain. She was awake, and the water bottle was mostly empty. When she said she needed to use the bathroom, Owens took the cuff off her wrist and let her walk there alone. He stood by the door, waiting for her to finish, then led her back to the bed and re-attached the cuff.

"I'm going to put the blindfold on you again for your protection. I'll warn you now that if you take it off, you'll be able to identify us, and we'll have to kill you."

She said nothing.

"Do you want anything to eat?" He asked. "Just more water," she said softly.

He took last night's sandwich to the kitchen, threw it out, and returned with a fresh water bottle. After closing the door, he and Bruno sat down to make the call. When the receptionist put the call through to the attorney, Owens said in a modulated voice, "We have the girl. She is unhurt and will be returned when the lawsuit has been dropped."

"We will not discuss anything until Hannah speaks to her father. Can you call back at noon?" the attorney said.

"Noon it is," Owens replied and ended the call.

Since Bruno could only hear one side of the call, Owens said, "The girl's name is Hannah. We're going to let her speak to her father at noon."

"Are they going to drop the lawsuit?"

"Most likely. First, they want to hear her voice."

"I get it," Bruno said.

They turned on the TV, scanning through the local news channels for any mention of the kidnapping. At noon, Bruno suggested, "Maybe we should make the call a few minutes late. That will make the father go crazy."

"I like it," Owens replied. "I can just imagine him pacing the room, tearing his hair out," They called at 12:15, with Hannah blindfolded and cuffed to a chair next to them at the table. When the attorney was on the line, Owens said, "So, have you agreed to drop the lawsuit?"

The attorney asked to hear Hannah's voice, so Owens disconnected the modulator and whispered for Hannah to speak. After she said a few words,

Owens snatched the phone from her and reconnected the modulator before saying, "See? We haven't hurt her."

The attorney said, "We'll drop the case immediately. Where can we pick her up?"

"As soon as we can confirm that the lawsuit has been withdrawn, we'll call back—maybe tomorrow," he said before ending the call.

Bruno led Hannah back to the bedroom, placed the open cuff around the bedpost, then closed the door and returned to the table. "How long will it take them to withdraw the lawsuit?" he asked.

"It shouldn't take too long. I'll call the town clerk's office later this afternoon," Owens replied.

When they made sandwiches for lunch, Owens took one to Hannah's door, peeked in to ensure she had the blindfold on, and placed it on the chair.

"Are you hungry?" he asked. "No," she replied.

"I'll just leave it here if you change your mind."

Owens and Bruno played cards until Owens announced he was taking a nap. They were both tired from sleeping in shifts the previous night. While Owens was sleeping, Bruno went in to check on Hannah, who was also sleeping. He watched the young woman for a while, sleeping peacefully, with her chest rising slightly with each breath. He became aroused. He moved closer and put a hand on one of her breasts, gently squeezing. When he moved his hand to her other breast, she awoke startled, and realizing why, she blindly swung her free hand and caught Bruno flush in the face. Now, he was the startled one.

The noise was loud enough to wake Owens, and he came in to see what was going on. When he saw Bruno standing over the girl with the left side of his face bright red, he knew what happened.

"Jesus Christ, were you trying to feel her titties?"

"I guess I was."

"Leave her the fuck alone. I have a daughter that age!"

They both entered the living room, and Owens called the White Plains town clerk. Without identifying himself, he asked if attorney Seth Bodner had withdrawn a lawsuit that day. When told he had, Owens thanked the clerk and ended the call. "It's done. We're all set," he announced.

Detective Kidd and Sean O'Riley arrived just a few moments apart but in separate cars. They walked in with a cooler and a bag of Chinese take-out.

"Hey, guys," O'Riley said. "Did they drop the lawsuit?"

"Yes, they did. I just confirmed it with the town clerk," Owens said.

As Owens and Bruno were preparing to leave, Owens said, "We'll be back in the morning and figure out what to do with her then. Her name is Hannah, by the way."

Once they were gone, O'Riley opened the bag of Chinese food, took out an egg roll, and brought it to Hannah. With her still blindfolded, he said, "Here's an egg roll."

"I'm not hungry, but I need to pee," she said. "When I finish dinner, I'll take you to the bathroom."

He returned to the table, opened a beer, and shared the bag of Chinese food with Kidd. A half-hour later, he returned to Hannah's room and asked, "Do you still need to pee?"

She nodded.

"If I'm going to do something for you, you need to do something for me."

"Like what?"

"Show me your tits," he smiled.

Imagining his sleazy smile but realizing an escape opportunity might present itself, she said, "Fine. Unhook me from this bed."

O'Riley's smile grew larger as he unlocked the handcuff and backed up for the viewing. Hannah lifted her shirt and bra together, exposing her breasts, hoping he would come closer. When he didn't move, she asked, "Would you like to touch them?"

His eyes widened, and he stepped closer. When she felt his hands on her breasts, she kneed him in the balls with all the power she could muster. He immediately hunched over in pain as the air rushed out of his lungs. As he collapsed to the floor, she pulled her shirt down, removed the blindfold, and ran out of the room, heading for the front door. With the doorknob in her hand, she turned it and began to pull the door open when Kidd tackled her from behind.

He wrestled her to the floor, pulled her arms behind her back, and placed his knee on her neck. As athletic as she was, she was no match for his immense weight. In this position, she could barely breathe and felt more helpless and defeated than she ever had in her life.

A minute later, O'Riley came crawling out of the bedroom on his hands and knees, and Kidd started laughing, releasing his knee from her neck. As she gasped for air, he picked her up, led her back to the bedroom, and hooked her up to the bed. She could still see O'Riley writhing in pain, calling her every curse word she had ever heard. Whatever satisfaction she got from seeing him in pain quickly vanished as she realized that she could now identify her captors, and that might have been her only chance at escape.

As it became darker, she fell asleep feeling hopeless.

CHAPTER 26

Dan Burnett

On my way to New-Ro, I updated Frosty and Seth on the new developments. They both agreed with Jim and my conclusion that Hannah was being held at the cottage in Danbury. Frosty was gung-ho about going up to rescue her, while Seth wanted to wait for her release. I agreed with both of them. We would wait out the day, and if we didn't get her back, we would go up and get her.

When I arrived at Sheila's, she and Frank were anxious for any news. I filled them in on the discovery of where we thought Hannah was being held and about our plan to wait out the day in the hope she was released. If that did not happen, we would plan a rescue.

"They said they would release her today if you dropped the case. Did you?" she asked.

"Yes. Seth filed the withdrawal yesterday afternoon. I'm sure the word has spread throughout the department by now."

"Then I'm still hopeful they will release her."

"Me too. We're just making a contingency plan if they don't."

She nodded her head without saying a word. When I rose to leave, she hugged me before I walked out the door while Frank followed me out.

"Listen, If you are planning a raid, I want in. That's the type of mission I was trained for and carried out many times in Afghanistan."

"Okay. Your experience would be helpful. If we do it, I'll get someone else to stay with Sheila."

"Good. Thanks, Dan."

Having nothing to do except wait for Seth's call, I returned to the boat to rest in case I pulled another all-nighter. Once aboard, I checked my emails and saw one from Mia. I couldn't believe it, but that was the first time I had thought about her in two days. Her email was mostly about everything they were doing and how much she missed me. I wondered if I should tell her about Hannah being kidnapped and recalled her telling me not to keep things from her. I feared she might never forgive me if I didn't tell her, but I felt it was not something to say in an email—she'd have a million questions and be beside herself. I checked the time and determined it was six p.m. in Portugal, which is as good a time as any to try a phone call.

"Dan? Is that you?"

"Yes, sweetheart. Are you having a good time?"

"We absolutely love it here. You have to come with me next time."

"I just read your email, and it reminded me how much I miss you."

"I miss you too, love. How is the case going?"

"Are you in a good place to talk?"

"Yes, we're in the hotel room. You sound serious, Dan."

"Hannah has been kidnapped, and her bodyguard was shot."

"Oh my god! I'll come right home."

"No, don't do that. The last thing I need is to worry about you, too!"

"What happened?"

I told her about the last few days' events: dropping the case, hoping for her release, and tracking the bad cops to the cottage. I did not mention any plans of a rescue that would worry her further.

"What are you going to do?"

"Right now, I'm waiting for her release. I'm not sure what I'll do if she's not."

"Are you sure you don't want me there? I don't think I can enjoy myself worrying about Hannah. And you!"

"Yes, I'm sure. I'll let you know the minute we get her back."

"Okay, call me anytime. I'll keep my phone beside me night and day."

"I will, sweetheart. Try to enjoy your trip."

"That won't be possible until I know Hannah is safe."

"I know. But try anyhow.

"Okay, Dan. I love you."

"I love you, too, Mia."

I sat back on the settee and weighed the bomb I had just dropped on her, second-guessing my decision to tell her. Like all second guesses, it was water under the bridge.

Waiting to hear from Seth was making me crazy. Whenever I closed my eyes, I could only imagine what Hannah might be going through, and my anger grew. I thought of all kinds of things I would do to those cops if Hannah was hurt in any way. I thought of gruesome torture and painful death that I would put every one of them through. I must have slept at some point because those dreams had become too vivid. It was after 3:00 when I awoke, and I still had not heard from Seth.

I called his office, and when Paula answered, I said, "Anything?"

"I'm sorry, Dan. Nothing yet. I promise we'll let you know the moment they call."

"Okay, Paula. Thanks."

I realized it was time for Plan B and called Frosty on his cell.

"Anything, Dan?"

"Nothing. I think it's time for us to go get her before they change their minds about releasing her."

"I agree. I've been thinking about this all day. Maybe it's time I put my SWAT team training to use."

"Frank wants in on this, too. He says he did this stuff in Afghanistan with the Marines."

"Good. Previous experience is worth its weight in gold."

"Let's meet at Sheila's at 5:30. I'll call Jim, and we'll have a planning session with Frank."

I called Jim to inform him of our meeting and then called Dave to tell him his guard duty tonight would be at Sheila's house in New-Ro. With all that organized, I let Frank know I was on my way.

When I arrived, Sheila looked at me with hope in her eyes that I had good news. I shook my head and said, "I'm sorry, nothing yet."

Frank and I went into the garage to begin our planning session. I described the cottage as best I could from my brief drive-by and asked how he envisioned the raid taking place.

"We should go in after one a.m. when whoever is guarding her will be struggling to stay awake. We'll kick in the front and back doors, use a couple of Flash Bang grenades to disorientate them, and storm the house. If any of them have a weapon in their hands, shoot to kill. We'll search the rooms for Hannah, lead her out, and drive away. We should have two cars if someone needs to stay behind to deal with unforeseen issues. That's pretty much it—in and out. The quicker, the better."

"What weapons will we be using?"

"Whatever each of us is comfortable with. Let's see what the other guys bring with them. I'll have an M-27 that I used in the Marines—a semi-automatic assault rifle with a scope. I can spray it around in close quarters and also use it long-range as a sniper rifle. At some point this evening, I need to go to the shop and pick up the Flash Bangs."

"I'm most comfortable with my service pistol, a Glock-19," I said. "Do we know how many guys are in the house with her?"

"No. We should plan for two, though. I only saw one vehicle in the driveway, and we observed one person leave when another arrived by tracking two of their vehicles."

It was about that time that Jim and Frosty showed up. Sheila led them out to the garage and asked if we would be ready to eat in an hour. We all nodded, and she went back inside. After introducing everyone, Frank reviewed the plan as we discussed it, and Frosty said it sounded very similar to his SWAT team training.

He asked, "How many doors are there, and how many of us are going in?"

"I saw a front door, and I assume there's a back door, although it might be sliding glass in the back because the cottage has a view of the lake," I said.

"It might be a little crowded if we all go in," Frank said. "How about I stay outside and handle anyone who runs out? I have my share of marksman badges, and with the scope, I can take someone out through a window."

Jim, seeming excited to participate in the action, said, "I brought a shotgun—a good weapon to take someone down without aiming. I'll have a Glock, too."

"Same here," Frosty said.

"Would you guys like an armored vest and helmet? We have them at the shop," Frank asked.

We looked at each other, and all nodded our heads.

"Done. When we get there, we'll scope out the cottage to see if we can identify where people are, and we'll make any last-minute adjustments then," Frank concluded.

"Sounds like a plan. Let's see what Sheila made us for dinner," I said, knowing that cooking for us was her way of contributing. She was old school in that regard.

We walked inside with a bit of an adrenaline pump in anticipation of our rescue plan. Sheila had set the table with a basket of bread and had a pot of beef stew on the stove, ready to go. After serving us, she joined us at the table with a small plate for herself, and Jim and Frosty got to know Frank a little better, asking him about his experience serving in Afghanistan. Sheila seemed fascinated by his stories.

After dinner, Frank asked if anyone needed anything else from the shop at the security building. We told him no, and as he walked out to his car, Dave arrived. I saw them chat for a few minutes before Dave entered the house. I introduced him to everyone, and Sheila asked if he had eaten. When he said he had not, she set him a place at the table, served him some stew, and sat with him, chatting while Frosty and I did the dishes.

When Frank returned with the gear, we each tried on the vests and helmets, making adjustments before claiming a spot to nap before our planned departure at midnight.

CHAPTER 27

f I slept at all, it was briefly. I pictured different scenarios of what we would face that evening and how we would deal with them. From my experience, no matter how much you planned, an event like this could go entirely differently from what you thought. It was essential to be nimble and adjust in real time.

Around midnight, I heard people stirring. Frank was carrying the gear outside to be loaded into a car. Jim and Frosty were getting dressed and checking their ammo while Sheila filled two thermoses with coffee.

Ten minutes later, we were on the road. Frank rode with me in my car, and Frosty rode with Jim in his Highlander. We programmed each other's cell numbers into our phones, silenced our ringtones, and dimmed the screens. I sent out a group text that any of us could add to. That was the method we planned to use to coordinate our attack. After checking the tracking app, I saw that O'Riley's Mustang was at the cottage, and Bruno's Pickup was in Tarrytown. I shared that info in the group text.

The night was particularly dark, with just a sliver of moonlight, and the temperature was cool but not too cold. Approaching the cottage from Bear Mountain Road would cause our headlights to shine directly into it, so I advised Jim to follow us, turn off the headlights when we did, and park the car for a fast escape. Just before the last curve on Bear Mountain, before the intersection of Rocky Point, I shut off the headlights and stopped a few hundred yards short of the cottage. It was a desolate area, just dense woods on both sides of the road. I turned off the dome light before opening the door, and we put our vests and helmets on before approaching the cottage.

We saw both the Mustang and the Explorer parked in the driveway. In the front yard, there was a large tree with some bushes on one side that we huddled behind. It appeared there was some dim light inside, with a bluish glow that flickered occasionally from a TV in the living area on the left. We assumed the front door opened into the living area. Now that we had all seen the cottage, we formulated a plan, whispering as softly as possible. Frank wanted to stay right there between the tree and the bushes, as it gave him a perfect sightline to the front door. We wanted more detail on the interior layout, so Frosty, Jim, and I walked along the right side of the cottage, away from the driveway, staying on the grass so as not to make any noise from stepping on sticks or leaves.

Judging from the window styles, there appeared to be two bedrooms on the right side. When we reached the rear, we saw a ground-level deck along the entire backside, with a kitchen door in the middle and a sliding glass door on the far side, away from the bedrooms. Once we made it around the far side, we met up with Frank to finalize our plan.

I would go in the front door, and Jim and Frosty would go in the back while Frank stayed put. As soon as we kicked in the doors, we would roll the Flash Bangs into the room, one in front and one in back. Frank reminded us to kick hard on the doorknob side. Once inside, we would neutralize whoever we saw, then search for Hannah and get her out. By now, our eyes had become accustomed to the dark, and we all felt there was enough light inside to operate. Frank agreed to send out the GO text once we were in place.

I gave Jim and Frosty a minute's head start before I took my place by the front door. A few moments later, I felt my phone vibrate. I kicked in the door and rolled in the Flash Bang. As it went off, I heard the other one from the backdoor—they were louder and brighter than I expected, and then everything went into slow motion. With my Glock raised, I entered the living area, saw O'Riley reclined on the couch, appearing disorientated, and saw Jim and Frosty head for the bedrooms. O'Riley's gun was on his lap, and when he picked it up, I shot him in the chest. He looked at me in disbelief, and while returning the stare, I shot him again in the forehead from inches away, causing his body to convulse once and drop the weapon. A moment later, when he was lifeless, I followed my partners toward the bedrooms and saw them frozen in place. Beyond them, I saw William Kidd holding a gun to Hannah's head.

"One move, and she's dead," he shouted. "Drop your weapons and back away."

We did precisely what he said. He had one arm around Hannah's neck while holding a pistol to her head with the other hand, and I could see she was terrified with her eyes opened wide. As we backed up, he followed us out of the bedroom and into the living area, away from the front door. They remained facing us as he backed toward the door. Hannah's eyes were locked on mine while we watched every move. Kidd's gun lowered a few inches as they went through the doorway and onto the front stoop. There was a crack of sound, and in that same instant, his head exploded, spraying blood and brain matter everywhere.

As his torso collapsed, Hannah went down with it and fell into the bushes; I ran to her, picked her up, and held her. She clung to me, dazed and shaking.

The entire encounter lasted way less than a minute, but I had her—alive and well. She started sobbing and clung to me tightly as we walked to the car. Frank was waiting for us with the engine running, ready to go. As Hannah and I climbed into the back seat, Frosty tossed us some towels before we drove away. After moistening one with water, I used them to wipe the blood and gore from her face as she continued shaking. After a few minutes, I offered her a bottle of water. Initially, she only took a few small sips but then drank the whole bottle, and her shaking stopped.

"Is Kristine alive?" she asked.

"Yes, Han. She's in the hospital, and she's going to make it," I answered, sensing another level of relief from her.

Once we were on Route 684, heading home with Jim and Frosty behind us, I called Sheila. She answered on the first ring.

"We have her. Safe and sound."

"Let me hear her voice!"

I handed the phone to Hannah, and she said, "I'm okay, Mom. We'll be home soon." Then, unable to continue the conversation, she returned the phone to me.

"That's probably enough for now, Sheila; I'll have her home in a half-hour. Oh, she'll need a shower first thing."

A few minutes later, Frosty called. "How is she?"

"I think she's still in shock, but I got her to drink some water, and she talked to her mom."

"Wonderful. Jim and I gathered all the weapons. We need to discuss informing the Danbury Police."

"Yeah, we do. Maybe we should let Seth handle it."

"Sounds good to me. We'll see you back at the house. I need to get my car and give you back your gun. Frank might want his gear back as well."

"Okay, buddy. See you soon."

When we arrived at the house, Sheila ran out into the driveway to greet Hannah and took her into the house. I felt it best to leave them to each other and stay out of their way. I gathered with the guys for a beer in the garage, and we went through a brief replay of how it went down. The events were still raw, and we were all too tired for a whole male bonding thing. Jim and Frosty took off a few minutes later, and I thanked Frank for all he had done. I then headed to the marina for some rest aboard Privateer. While driving, the letdown from the adrenaline rush finally set in, and I felt exhausted.

Once aboard, I collapsed on my bunk, closed my eyes, and remembered my promise to call Mia. The connection took a few moments, but I heard her voice: "Dan?"

"Yes, It's me, sweetheart. We have her—it's over."

"Oh, that's such a relief."

"We killed two people, though, so we may face some legal issues."

"Who's we?"

"Jim, Frosty, and Sheila's security guard, Frank."

"Oh my god! Did you do like a SWAT team raid?"

"Pretty much. The important thing is we got her back, alive and well."

"That's so good to hear."

"Well, it's still the middle of the night here, and I need some sleep."

"I'll let you go then. I love you."

"Love you, too."

Before climbing into my bunk, I texted Seth and asked him to call me when he was up and around. Then, finally, I got some sleep.

CHAPTER 28

Just as the sun rose, my phone rang—it was Seth. "Good morning, Dan. I got your message."

"We got Hannah back last night."

"That's fantastic! Do I want to know how you did that?"

"Yeah, you need to hear it because we need your help. We killed two of the kidnappers, O'Riley and Kidd."

"I'm all ears."

I told him how it happened, down to the smallest detail. He never interrupted and only spoke once I was done when I asked him how we should handle the Danbury police.

"Let me deal with it. First, I'll check and see if they even know about it yet, then I'll speak to the U.S. Attorney and see if he wants the FBI to take it from here. So long as the locals know we're cooperating with the FBI, they might just let it go."

"The scene was pretty ugly, Seth. I can't imagine it not making the news."

"I'm sure you're right about that. I'll let you know how I do; just sit tight for now."

"Oh. The address was 3 Rocky Point."

"Okay, thanks for that. Congratulations."

After I made coffee, I called Sheila and asked how Hannah was doing. "I was up with her most of the night, but she's sleeping now. They molested her, Dan. She says they didn't rape her, just squeezed her breasts and things like that. She's going to need to talk to a therapist about this."

"I agree. Do you want to set that up, or would you like me to?"

"I don't know anyone," she said.

"I know someone who does. At the department, we referred victims to therapists all the time."

"All right, I'll leave it to you."

"Okay. How are you doing?"

"I'm so relieved to have her back. Frank told me what you guys did; it sounds like something from a movie."

"It was. Frank played an important part in this."

"It sounds like you all did. Thank you, Dan. And please thank Jim and Matt for me."

"I will. Let Frank know that Attorney Bodner is handling the police, at least for now."

"Will do. I'll let Hannah know you called."

"Thanks."

Nothing was on the morning news about the mess we left in Danbury. I checked the Internet and found nothing there either. I wondered if it was possible that it was still undiscovered. Surely, someone must have heard the shots. I texted Frosty and Jim, telling them that Seth would inform the Danbury Police and that I would keep them posted. Then, I called Anne Gibbs, my psychologist friend, for a referral for Hannah.

"Hi, Dan. How's everything?"

"Well, I have a problem I hope you can help with, Anne."

"I will if I can."

"My daughter was kidnapped, and we just got her back last night. It was a violent scene, and she should talk to somebody. Can you recommend someone?"

"That's just awful. Is she okay?"

"Yeah, just a bit shook up."

"I recommend Lisa Robbins. She's really good with young women and trauma like this. I'll text you her number."

"Thanks. Did Attorney Bodner contact you about the racist cop?"

"He did. I'm supposed to meet with him next week."

"Well, I'm not sure I should be telling you this, but that appointment just got canceled. Sean O'Riley is no longer alive."

"Oh my god! Was he involved with the kidnapping?"

"He was. You'll probably hear all about it on the evening news."

"Thanks for the information, Dan. I hope everything works out with your daughter."

"Me, too. Thanks, Anne."

After receiving Lisa Robbins' contact information and forwarding it to Sheila, I called her. "How's Hannah?"

"Not good. She woke up a little bit ago and took another shower. She says she keeps feeling the guy's brains dripping from her hair—she's really freaked out."

"I can understand that. Maybe we should see if the shrink can see her today."

"I'll call her right now," she said.

"Good. Use Anne Gibbs' name as who referred you."

"Okay, I'll let you know how I make out."

After ending that call, I saw a new text from Seth saying, "Call me." When I did, Paula put me right through.

"Dan, thanks for calling back."

"How are we looking?"

"The U.S. Attorney for the Southern District has asked the FBI to investigate everything. The racist cops, the kidnapping, your rescue, everything. Because the kidnapping was interstate, that's automatically the FBI's jurisdiction. The Special Agent at the Westchester Field Office contacted the Danbury Police late this morning. They knew nothing about what happened last night until he told them."

"I can't believe no one heard the shots or the grenades and called it in."

"That must be a pretty rural area."

"It's in a valley by a lake, all hills and woods. Maybe the sound echoed, and no one knew where it originated."

"Listen, the FBI wants to talk to you—today, and I'd like to be present when they do. How soon can you be here?"

"I'll leave right now. Let's say an hour?"

"Good, I'll set it up. Tell your buddies to expect a call from the Feebs, and I recommend they have an attorney present when speaking with them."

"Okay, see you in a bit."

Before leaving, I called Jim, Frank, and Frosty and told them that the Danbury Police had been informed and that the FBI would be calling them. I also told them about Seth's recommendation that they have an attorney present when speaking with them. We also discussed what to say to the Feebs, and I was adamant about telling them everything as we remembered it. There was no reason to get cute and leave something out—that would make them suspicious if our testimonies were inconsistent.

When I walked into Seth's office, the Agents were waiting for me in the conference room. Seth and I joined them, and they introduced themselves.

"Hello, Mr. Burnett. I'm John Meyers, the Special Agent in charge of the Westchester field office, and this is Agent Charles Logan. May we call you Dan?"

"That's fine," I replied, feeling a bit on guard. Even though I had been a cop for thirty years and had no sense of guilt whatsoever, being interviewed by

J. Edgar Hoover's FBI got my attention.

"We have seen everything attorney Bodner shared with the US attorney and know about these cop's previous activities. How about you tell us about the kidnapping of your daughter and the rescue?"

I began my account when I became aware of being followed and hiring security guards to protect Hannah and her mother. I told them everything that happened up until today. It took nearly two hours to tell the whole story, while they stopped me from time to time with questions about my rescue team and our use of firearms. As I told the story, I became aware that they might think we acted as vigilantes, and I was concerned about how this looked for Frosty. As an active cop, he was responsible for following the book and notifying his superiors of what he was doing. I doubted he had done that.

When the interview wrapped up, we exchanged contact information, and as we were shaking hands, Special Agent Meyers said, "Congratulations on rescuing your daughter."

I was mildly relieved to hear they understood what was at stake for me.

Once they were gone, Seth and I chatted about how it went and where he thought it would go from there.

"After interviewing the rest of your team, they'll want to talk to Hannah."

"She's not ready for that. She's having nightmares, and we're trying to get her to speak with a shrink, hopefully today."

"That's certainly understandable. I'll make sure they go through me before interviewing her."

"Good. Do you think we need to keep the bodyguards in place?"

"Yeah, maybe now more than ever. I'll be concerned until all of them are in custody. Do you want someone new for Hannah?"

"Maybe, although I think Frank can handle it as long as she's home. I'll speak to him and let you know."

On my way home, I called Frank and asked him his thoughts on guarding the house by himself.

"I'll be okay for a day or two so long as Hannah and Sheila are together.

After that, I'll need some help at night so I can sleep."

"Okay, I'll work on that tomorrow."

"Sheila wants me to tell you she has an appointment with the shrink in the morning. I'll drive them."

"Thanks, Frank."

When I returned to Privateer, I popped open a beer and called Frosty. I told him about my interview and asked If he thought he would get blowback from the NYPD about getting involved.

"I might, but what the hell. That was an emergency situation, and we rescued a kidnapping victim!" he exclaimed.

"I hope Chief Blaisdale sees it that way."

"If he doesn't, screw him. What's the worst they can do? Suspend me for a week or two? I can use some time off."

"I'm glad you feel that way, Matt."

"By the way, the Feebs called and want to see me tomorrow. The union attorney will arrange the time and place."

"Sheila asked me to thank you for last night."

"I was happy to be part of it, Dan. Give Hannah a hug for me."

"Will do, pal."

I called Jim, told him about my interview with the FBI, and asked if he had heard from them.

"Not yet. How about I come by the marina, and we'll celebrate last night's success?"

"Sure. I could use a celebration right about now."

"Great. I'll see you in an hour."

When he arrived, I saw him walking down the ramp with a package. Once I had let him in the gate and we had climbed aboard, he handed it to me. It was a ten-year-old bottle of Basil Hayden Bourbon.

I poured a small glass with ice for each of us, and we sat in the cockpit overlooking the marina while sipping our drinks. After asking about Hannah, he spoke about how good for business it would be when word got out that our PI agency exposed a group of white supremacist cops and also rescued a kidnapping victim. I hadn't given that any thought, but he was absolutely right.

When our glasses were empty, we went below for a refill, and I gave him a tour of the boat. While below, I turned on the TV to see if last night's rescue had made the news yet. It certainly had!

The network cameras not only showed two bodies covered with sheets but also showed all the blood and gore around the busted doorway. The reporter said the FBI was handling the investigation. Neither Jim nor I would typically celebrate a loss of life, but in this case, having rescued my daughter from some evil men, we touched glasses and said, "Cheers."

Dave showed up before dark, and over the next few hours, we cooked burgers on the marina's grill and told him about the rescue. He drank Coke while Jim and I continued with bourbon and beer, exceeding my usual limit. By the end of the evening, Jim and I were pretty well-snockered, so I sent him home in an Uber.

CHAPTER 29

I climbed out of my bunk the following morning, nursing a hangover—not a bad one, but enough that I was moving a little slow. Dave was already gone for the day but had left a warm pot of coffee on the stove. While I was having my second cup, Willy Grant called.

"Did I hear correctly that you went in like SEAL Team Six went after Bin Laden?"

"Well, no helicopters," I laughed.

"Jesus, Dan, you're supposed to be retired!"

"I know, I know. What can I say?"

"I guess you were properly motivated."

"You could say that, for sure," I laughed again. "How's Hannah?"

"Physically fine, but she's seeing a shrink today. I hope to talk with her later."

"Well, I hope she'll be okay. Let's have a beer one of these days—I'm dying to hear all about it."

"You got it. Thanks for the call."

While eating a bowl of cereal, I turned on the TV and saw Captain Owens of the WPPD being perp-walked by the FBI. The reporter said he owned the cottage in Danbury where the rescue had occurred.

I called Seth to arrange an additional bodyguard at Sheila's house, and we discussed Owens's arrest. As the cottage owner, we agreed he was low-hanging fruit, but Seth had no new information on the other cops.

When he texted me the confirmation for the additional bodyguard, I forwarded it to Frank. He called me a few minutes later.

"Hi, Dan. I know Jenifer, the guard they're sending tonight. She's good; I've worked with her before, and Hannah will like her."

"Good to hear. Has Hannah been to see Lisa Robbins yet?"

"Her appointment is at eleven. We'll be leaving shortly. The FBI called and would like to interview me today. I'm letting my company arrange an attorney, so I'm unsure of the time."

"Great. Keep me posted."

"I will. Bye, Dan."

A lot was going on today. I went up to the cockpit, hoping to sort it all out. For a weekday, there was a fair amount of activity in the marina. A few small boats of retired guys were heading out with fishing poles and bait buckets. It was a perfect day for it, sunny and mild with barely a breeze.

As I organized my thoughts, I was most focused on Hannah and the shrink, Lisa Robbins, and was anxious to hear how it went. I saw Jim being dropped off in the parking lot by his wife to retrieve his car. I wandered up the ramp to say hello, and she thanked me for not letting Jim drive home last night. We chatted for a few minutes, and Jim told me he had an interview with the FBI and his attorney scheduled for the following day. He wasn't expecting any problems, and I was happy to hear that everyone had taken Seth's advice. We talked about Captain

Owens' arrest and wondered about the others before they drove away. I wandered back to the boat and resumed my perch in the cockpit, observing the activity.

Sheila called a few minutes later with an update on Hannah. "She's in rough shape emotionally, Dan. I can see it in her face; her eyebrows are always scrunched."

"Was Lisa able to help at all?"

"I think so. I saw her smile a little on the way out, and she'll see her again tomorrow. It was traumatic for her to see Kristine get shot and then be hand-cuffed to a bed for two days and molested. Not to mention having a gun held to her head and being covered in gore."

"My God. When you spell it out like that, I feel terrible for her. I hope she can put all that behind her."

"Me, too."

"Did Frank tell you about the new bodyguard?"

"Yes. I think she's coming later this afternoon so Frank can concentrate on his interview."

"Are they doing it at your house?"

"Sounds like it. Frank did not want us to be alone, so his attorney set it up to be done here."

"All right. Tell Hannah I'd like to see her when she's ready."

"I will. Bye, Dan."

After eating a sandwich in the cockpit, I laid back and closed my eyes, reliving the last few days' events. I still felt exhausted from the overnights and emotionally drained. I must have slept because the sun was low on the horizon when my phone rang.

"Hey, Frosty. How was your day?"

"Great. The interview with the Feebs was a piece of cake, and Captain Craig and Chief Blaisdale think I'm a hero."

"Excellent! I'm glad this didn't go badly for you."

"How's Hannah?"

"I'm not sure. Sheila says she's pretty shaken up, but she saw a shrink today and is seeing her again tomorrow. We're hoping for the best."

"Well, I'll be pulling for her."

"Thanks for the call, Matt."

When Dave arrived that evening, he and I went to the diner for something to eat, and I was happy not to dine alone. We chatted more about the rescue and Captain Owens's arrest, then wandered back to the boat.

When I turned on the TV, there was a breaking news report linking the kidnapping and the rescue in Danbury to the White Plains Police Department. They said that in addition to Captain Owens, the two dead men in Danbury were WPPD officers and that some other officers had been suspended pending further investigation.

After seeing that, I went to bed comfortable with our accomplishment while Dave played night watchman again.

"Dan, you'll want to see this," Dave announced, tapping my shoulder.

I sat up, rubbed my face, and saw it was nearly eight a.m. I wandered out to the salon in my boxer shorts to see more cops being perp-walked on television.

Dave poured me a coffee as I listened to the reports of Captain Johnson and Officer McGhee's early morning arrests. According to the reporter, the arrests occurred before sunrise, and they were still asleep. You got to hand it to the FBI—they know how to make a dramatic arrest.

After that, Dave took off, and I dressed for the day. An hour later, Seth called.

"I assume you've seen the news reports this morning?" he asked.

"Yeah, the only one left is Bruno."

"I wonder why."

"Maybe they just haven't found him yet. Maybe he's on the run."

"Could be. I'll ask Agent Meyers if that's the case," Seth said. "All right, let me know what he says."

"I'll be in touch."

Immediately after ending the call, I remembered I still had a tracking device on Bruno's pickup. I opened the app and saw the icon in a shopping center parking lot near his house in Tarrytown. I wondered if I should notify Agent Meyers that I could track that vehicle. I knew it was illegal for citizens to stalk someone with a tracking device, but maybe he'd like to know. I thought I'd wait until I heard from Seth and bounce it off him.

A few minutes later, he called back.

"Agent Meyers says they have a warrant for Bruno's arrest, but he wasn't home this morning. They expect to locate him soon."

"I never told you this, but I have a tracking device on one of Bruno's vehicles—the Toyota pickup. It's in a parking lot near his house at the moment."

"The courts have been decisive that those are illegal without a warrant. It could taint evidence in a trial and cause a case to be thrown out."

"I know. That's why I kept it to myself. Do you think Meyers would like to know about it?"

"Why don't you ask him? I'd rather not be involved."

"Okay, I have his contact info. I'll call him."

"Good. Let's keep our bodyguards in place until this is finished."

"Yup. Bye, Seth."

I called the cell phone number that Agent Meyers gave me. He answered on the first ring, "This is Meyers."

"Hello, John; this is Dan Burnett calling."

"Yes, Dan. What can I do for you?"

"I understand you are looking for Sergeant Bruno, and I wanted to let you know I can track his pickup truck. Would you like that information?"

"I appreciate the call, Dan, but I can't use that without a warrant. If we don't locate him soon, we'll get a warrant and put our own devices on his vehicles."

"Okay. I just thought I should let you know."

"Thanks anyway, Dan."

I grabbed a bacon and egg sandwich and a cup of coffee to go at the diner and headed to Tarrytown, driving on Westchester County's myriad of parkways to eyeball Bruno's pickup. The tracking app led me to the front of a grocery store. Seeing only the Toyota and no signs of Bruno or his Chrysler, I drove by his house while I was nearby. There were no signs of his car there either, but it could have been in the garage. What I did notice, however, was a plain Chevy Malibu parked down the street under a shade tree with two people inside. As I drove by, I saw they fit the profile of FBI agents: one man and one woman in their late thirties, clean-cut with no facial piercings or neck tattoos. If I made them that quickly, I was sure Bruno could, too.

With nothing more to do in Tarrytown, I returned to City Island. Along the way, I checked in with Frank and asked how things were working out with the new bodyguard, Jenifer.

"All good on this end, Dan. She'll arrive before dark tonight; at least one of us will always be awake. We just returned from Hannah's appointment; I think she's napping."

"Good to hear. I assume you saw the arrests this morning?"

"Yeah, there's still one out there, so I guess I'll remain on the job for now?"

"That's correct. I'll be in touch."

"Bye, Dan."

I saw Hannah's face pop up on my phone later that afternoon. "Hi, Han, how are you feeling?"

"I'm better now that I've met with Lisa a couple of times."

"I'm happy to hear that."

"Thanks so much for getting me out of there, Dad."

"It was my fault that you were there in the first place. I was beside myself."

"You're too modest, Dad. You guys came in like the military."

"I guess we did. I was just so happy that you were alive," I stumbled with the last words as tears came to my eyes.

"I knew you would come for me. That's what kept me sane."

After weighing that, I said, "Let me know when you're up to seeing me."

"How about tomorrow? Can we go sailing?"

"For sure! Call me in the morning when you're ready."

"I'm looking forward to it!"

"Me too. Bye, Han. Love you!"

Buoyed by speaking with Hannah, I walked up to Sammy's for dinner at the bar. I went there occasionally to eat among other people, and there were always friendly faces looking for conversation among the bar crowd. After finishing, I wandered back to Privateer just as Dave was arriving. When he had completed his survey of the marina, we sat in the cockpit, enjoying the full moon on the horizon and its long reflection on the water. We chatted about the arrests this morning and Sergeant Bruno's unknown whereabouts. I told him about the tracking device I had placed on his pickup and opened the app to show him how it worked. Once it was opened, I handed him my phone so he could see for himself.

After zooming in and out for a few moments, he said, "The Icon appears to be moving," and handed the phone back to me.

After a quick look, I said, "You're right. We know where he is, but the FBI might not." I told him about Agent Meyers not wanting the tracking information from me. We watched him move around Tarrytown for a while, stopping occasionally before continuing on.

Eventually, I went to bed, looking forward to sailing tomorrow with Hannah. I tossed and turned for a while, then wondered about Bruno's location. I reopened the app to see where he was and found him on the Hutchinson River Parkway heading south—less than fifteen minutes from the marina.

I climbed out of the bunk, put on my pants, and told Dave we might have a visitor.

After I handed him my phone, he said, "It looks like he's heading right for City Island."

"Let's use this opportunity to devise a plan to deal with him if he indeed does come here," I said.

"The only reason he would be coming here is to do you harm."

"Agreed. We should split up—one of us on this boat and the other a few boats away."

As Dave checked his weapon, I retrieved mine from below while getting dressed. After rejoining Dave in the cockpit, I rechecked the app and saw Bruno on the City Island bridge. We were now sure he was coming for me.

"I'm going into the cockpit of that sport-fishing boat across the dock. How about you crouch low in this cockpit so he won't see you?"

"Okay, what's the plan?"

'Let's let him get all the way to the boat, and I'll surprise him and see what he does. If we have to shoot him, let's try not to kill him, but I want to stop him on the dock before he boards Privateer."

"Got it," I rechecked the app and saw that he was entering the parking lot. I informed Dave, climbed into the other boat, and crouched low in the cockpit, peeking over the rail with the top of my head hidden among fishing gear. Dave did the same on Privateer, hiding behind the helm. With the moonlit sky, we could easily see Bruno walk down the ramp and climb over the fence onto the floating dock. He continued toward the finger dock we were on, seeming to know which boat was mine. As he approached Privateer, he slowed, trying to see if anyone was up top. Seeing no one, he drew his handgun and cautiously approached the transom with his back to me.

I stood, took aim, and hollered, "Bruno! Freeze!"

Startled, he turned toward me with his weapon raised, and I shot him in the knee, causing him to fall into the water behind Privateer. Dave rushed to the transom with his gun pointed into the water as Bruno rose to the surface, gasping for air. We could no longer see a gun as he grabbed the dock with both hands.

Offering no assistance, we left him in the cold water, holding onto the dock, while I called Special Agent Meyers. It was just after midnight.

"Would you like to come by the marina and collect Sergeant Bruno?"

"Give me the address."

I did, and before ending the call, I said, "He might need some medical assistance."

Dave and I sat on Privateer, watching Bruno cling to the dock, shivering as the breeze picked up. It took a half hour for the Feebs to arrive. One was Agent Logan from my interview, and I thought I recognized the other from earlier that day in Tarrytown. They pulled Bruno from the water, saw what was left of his right knee, and called an ambulance. While waiting, his shivering intensified, and I handed him a blanket to wrap around himself as Agent Logan used Bruno's belt as a tourniquet around his thigh. He then asked me how this all went down. By the time I finished the story, the paramedics had arrived. They put Bruno on a gurney, loaded it into the ambulance, and drove away with the other agent riding with them. Agent Logan followed behind in his car.

"Would you like to celebrate your last night on the job with a little bourbon?" I asked Dave.

"Sounds good to me!"

While we enjoyed our drinks below in the warmth of the salon, I texted Seth that Bruno was in custody and we could let our bodyguards go. When we finished our drinks, we each got some well-deserved sleep.

CHAPTER 30

When Hannah called the following day, I was ready to go. After picking her up, we stopped to get sandwiches on our way back to the marina. I could easily see she was not her usual, cheerful self.

With her at the helm, I untied us and stowed the fenders while she steered Privateer into the Sound. Once we had cleared the channel and had some maneuvering room, I raised the sails, she shut down the engine, and we headed southeast on a close reach. While she was functioning, I still thought she looked distracted. Over the next few minutes, as she sat on the leeward side steering with her eyes on the tell-tales, I saw joy return to her face as she worked her way to windward, her hair flowing behind her.

We spoke very little, but with the tide heading out, we made it all the way to Northport by lunchtime. After we ate our sandwiches, Hannah went up on the foredeck to soak up some late April sunshine. When she had her fill, she returned to the cockpit smiling, gave me a peck on the cheek, and started the engine.

"Let's head back while there's still some wind," she said.

"Aye, aye, Cap," I said before going forward to raise the anchor.

The tide favored us on the return, too, and after our day on the water, I took her to Giuseppe's for dinner before dropping her off at home. I was joyous to see her smiling again, although I knew it would take time for her to heal.

I called Mia's cell phone the following morning. She and Judy were in the rental house in Lagos on the Algarve coast. We spoke for a long time, with me filling her in on the details of the last week, while she told me about all the places they had been and things she wanted to show me when I came back with her.

Throughout the conversation, it was always when I came back with her, never if I came back with her. That was fine with me; she was an experienced traveler and made everything sound beautiful. I told her about my plan to take the summer off and sail with her on an extended cruise to Newport and Block Island, or maybe Martha's Vineyard or Nantucket.

"Oh, Dan, that sounds wonderful. I can hardly wait!"

Eventually, when we considered the roaming charges, I let her go, but she said she would call me in a few days.

Over the next week, I planned our summer trip, making notes of places to stop and distances between them. I wanted our days to be leisurely, without having to sail or motor too long or hard to the next stop. I also prepared Privateer for an extended trip by doing all the scheduled service items and stocking up on everything we'd need.

One day, after visiting Kristine in the hospital, Hannah and I went sailing again. I filled her in on my summer plans and invited her to join us along the way. There were a few places she could drive to meet us and a few places she could take a ferry; it all depended on when she wanted to come. We also discussed her graduation day. She told me her mother was having a party for her and wanted to invite Mia and me.

"Are you sure she wants me to bring Mia?"

"Yes. I've told her about Mia, and she wants to meet her. Besides, I think she and Frank might have a thing going on. They've gone out to dinner a few times, and she talks to him on the phone every night. It's sort of cute to see her dating."

"I think that's wonderful, Han. I'm happy for her, and Frank is a great guy."

"Yeah, I think so, too."

Mia and I had been staying in touch by email every few days. When I told her about being invited to Hannah's graduation and Frank and Sheila dating, she was more surprised than I was. She had never met either one but said she was happy for them. A few days before her return, I offered to pick them up at JFK, and she thought it was great that Judy and I would finally meet.

The following day, I received a call from Seth. "HI, Dan. Are you all rested up?"

"I still have more to go," I laughed. "How is Hannah doing?"

"Pretty well, I think. She seems to like the shrink that Anne Gibbs recommended."

"That's good to hear. I don't mean to keep bugging you, but I'm calling to schedule Hannah for an interview with the FBI."

"When do they want to do it?"

"Sometime in the next week or so. Do you think she's ready for that? I'll be there with her, of course."

"I'll check with her and let you know first of the week."

"That should be fine."

"Good. Thanks, Seth."

"Bye, Dan. Enjoy your weekend."

According to the Delta Airlines website, Mia's flight would arrive on time. I parked in the cell phone waiting lot at JFK, anticipating her call. When she called and said they were at baggage claim, I drove to the Delta terminal and pulled to the curb. I saw Mia come through the exit with someone who looked a lot like her.

Despite the traffic cop directing everyone through, I got out and hugged Mia, and after an introduction, I hugged her sister, too. After placing their luggage in the back, I pulled away from the curb into a traffic mess. Once we were clear of the airport, Judy and I told each other how happy we were to meet finally. Glancing in the rearview mirror, the family resemblance was remarkable.

Judy was a few years older, a little heavier, and had graying hair, but the same effortless beauty and grace were there. I heard all about their trip on the way to her home in Chappaqua.

After I placed her bags inside the door, Mia and Judy hugged goodbye before we drove away toward Mia's house, holding hands the whole way.

Once inside, she put her arms around me, went up on her toes, and kissed me passionately. She led me upstairs and said, "You smell clean, but I need a shower. How about you get naked and into bed, and I'll ravage you when I'm done."

"Yes, Ma'am!"

She did exactly that, and we made love until dark, losing count of her orgasms. After laying in each other's arms for a while, we became hungry and went downstairs. The refrigerator was bare, but she found some steaks in the freezer. We let those thaw on the counter while enjoying a Manhattan in our happy place. Once the steaks were partially thawed, I put them on the grill while she made Spanish rice. We enjoyed our makeshift dinner with a glass of Cabernet while watching boat traffic on the Sound. When we finished eating, her body clock had caught up with her, and she began yawning. A few minutes later, she apologized and went to bed. By the time I had cleaned up and joined her, she was sound asleep.

The following day, we headed to the boat for a much-anticipated weekend. With the wind out of the north, we sailed across the Sound to Long Island and tied up in a slip at the marina in Glen Cove. After cocktails on the boat, we wandered up the dock to the Cove restaurant, where we shared fresh oysters and blackened red snapper.

Later, while lounging in the V-berth in post-coital bliss, I asked, "Would you like to do this all summer?"

"This is a whole new lifestyle for me, Dan. I'm loving it!"

"That's good. Tomorrow, I'll tell you about my plans."

She hugged me and snuggled into my neck, eventually falling asleep.

After breakfast, I spread my charts on the salon table and showed her all the places we could go. I told her I'd like Hannah to join us at some point and how she could get to different places to meet us. I also invited Judy to join us.

"That would be fantastic. I'm sure she would love Newport or Nantucket, or any of these places, for that matter. Plus, I want to show you off and get you to know each other. I'll call her tomorrow."

Later that morning, we headed back to City Island with her at the helm and me adjusting sails. Each time out, I hoped to teach her something new, and that day, I showed her how to navigate using the chart plotter. When Privateer was tied up at the marina, we relaxed in the cockpit for the rest of the afternoon, soaking in the sun and watching other boats return. Later, we strolled up to Sammy's for dinner. We spent the night aboard again, as she seemed to be getting comfortable with the marina lifestyle.

On Monday morning, while we were sipping coffee aboard Privateer, I remembered I needed to tell Seth when Hannah would be ready to speak with the FBI. I called her.

"Good morning, Dad. How was your weekend?"

"Great, Han. Mia and I sailed over to Glen Cove on Saturday and returned yesterday. We're still on board."

"I'm jealous!"

"We'll go out again soon, I promise."

"I have finals all week. But after graduation, I'm good to go."

"Great! I'm calling because the FBI wants to interview you about the kidnapping. Are you up for that?"

"Can it wait until after graduation?"

"Maybe. I'll find out and let you know. Attorney Bodner will be there to represent you. You'll just tell them the truth about what happened—it shouldn't be anything to worry about."

"Okay. I think I can handle it."

"I'm sure you can. How's it going with Lisa Robbins?"

"I like her. She convinced me that things weren't my fault and taught me ways to deal with my emotions. I hope I can continue to see her for a while."

"As long as you want, Han. I'm glad it's helping."

"It definitely is. By the way, I just spoke with Kristine; she's home now and recovering nicely. The doctors told her she should have no long-term effects."

"That's great to hear. Good luck with your finals; Mia and I look forward to seeing you graduate."

"Thanks, Dad. Love you!"

By midday, we were back at Mia's house. She spent the afternoon tending her garden. Now that it was the middle of May and the trees were starting to bloom, she was no longer fearful of a frost. She seemed to know what to plant and when—something I knew nothing about.

The following day, I called Seth to ask if Hannah's interview could wait until after graduation. He asked for the dates and said he would set it up. He informed me that Bruno was still in the hospital, and the others were out on bail, confined to their homes with ankle monitors. He felt they no longer posed any danger. When I asked him how long it would be before they went to trial, he said it would be at least until Labor Day before the case saw a courtroom. From experience, I knew it was not an excessively long time for our justice system to function, but I still felt impatient and frustrated.

Later that day, Sheila called and asked for Jim's contact information to invite him to the graduation party. She told me she had already invited Matt Frost and his wife Peg, whom she had met a few times over the years.

Over the next week, I didn't hear much from Hannah, as she was busy with finals and preparing for the graduation party. Mia and I had gone sailing again and spent the night on the boat, anchored in a peaceful little cove I knew about. We cooked lamb chops on a charcoal grill that hung off the stern rail and enjoyed a bottle of Malbec that I knew Mia liked. It was still too cold for swimming, but we looked forward to July when the water would be warmer.

Graduation Day was perfect: sunny and warm. It was held outdoors in the football stadium, where they had set up a stage for the presentation and chairs on the field for the students. Mia and I met Sheila and Frank outside so we could sit together. I had a little trepidation about Sheila's reaction to Mia, a woman younger than she, but she was gracious and welcoming. I then realized that her date, Frank, was younger still, so we were both on equal footing.

As we sat in the stands, Hannah spotted us and waved. She looked so happy with all of her friends in caps and gowns. After a well-received commencement address, they called the graduates up to receive their diplomas alphabetically. Hannah was one of the early ones on stage, and when we heard Magna Cum Laude after her name, the four of us cheered. When it was over, we wandered down to the field to congratulate her, and she introduced us to all her friends. We already knew her roommates and her boyfriend Ken, who had been sailing with us the previous year.

Later that afternoon, when Mia and I arrived at Sheila's house, we saw the party had already started. Hannah and her friends had ditched the caps and gowns and were dancing to a DJ on a portable dance floor under a huge white tent in the backyard. We saw Kristine had made it to the party and was dancing with Hannah's friends, having a good time.

Tables were set up with white tablecloths, along with a bar and bartenders. When we made our way there, we saw that Frosty, Peg, Jim, and his wife Nancy, had beaten us to it. Once we all had drinks in our hands, we found a table for the six of us. It wasn't long until Ken approached us, thanked us for rescuing Hannah, and told us how badass we all were.

When Sheila and Frank stopped by the table, Mia complimented her on the party arrangements. Hannah dragged me to the dance floor when the DJ played an oldie, and Mia and I danced together to the next song—everyone was having a great time. Later, when the catering staff set up the buffet, Sheila invited us all up to eat. They had supplied real plates and silverware with various offerings, including a carving station. It felt more like a wedding than a backyard party. A few hours later, Mia and I prepared to leave after congratulating Hannah and praising Sheila for the beautiful party. For the young people, it was just getting started.

Seth called Monday to inform me that Hannah's interview with the FBI would be the following day at ten a.m. I called and told her I would pick her up and drive her there. Even though I would have done that anyway, I thought it was time for her to get a car of her own.

On our way to Seth's office, I broached the subject with her, and she said, "Yes, I need a car, but they are crazy expensive nowadays. I have to wait until I land a job."

"Maybe I can help. I'll talk to your mother about it."

"Really? That would be awesome!"

"That can be your graduation present from me."

"She should be home all day. I think she's using up her vacation days."

"Good for her. Anyhow, about today's interview, I did mine a few weeks ago, and all they want is a true statement of what happened. Just take your time and tell them what you remember; don't try to fill in the blanks if you don't know. Seth will step in if it goes anywhere it shouldn't, and if something upsets you, he'll ask for a time-out so you can collect yourself."

"Okay, Dad. I'm sure I'll be fine."

I introduced her to everyone at the office, and Seth said he'd let me know when things were wrapping up. I assumed it would go until mid-afternoon like mine did. I knew they would not want me to have lunch with Hannah and coach her in the middle of the interview, so when lunchtime came, I went to Boonmee for some spicy chicken and noodles. After that, I wandered into Tibbets Park, sat on a bench, and called Sheila while enjoying the warmth of the midday sun.

"Hello, Dan."

"Hi, Sheila. That was a fantastic party you threw for Hannah. We had a great time!"

"I'm glad you enjoyed it. How is her interview going?"

"I don't know, but I would assume fine; Seth is in the room with her."

"I'm happy to hear that."

"Hey, I wanted to do something for Hannah as a graduation present.

Maybe I'll buy her a used car If you're okay with that."

"Sounds good to me. She needs a car, and that would be a big help."

"Okay. I'll have her home in a few hours."

"Bye, Dan."

Having nothing else to do, I wandered up to Seth's office and chatted with Paula and Linda until Hannah finished. Less than an hour later, the door opened, and Special Agent Meyers and Agent Logan walked out. They nodded toward me in recognition and left the office. A moment later, Hannah and Seth came out smiling, Seth praising her performance.

On the way home, I told Hannah I had received her mother's blessing to buy her a car.

"Are you sure you can afford it? I know you're retired now."

"I'm semi-retired, Han. The PI thing has been working out so far. I know a used car guy in the Bronx who gives all cops good deals; that's where I got this one. How about we see if he has anything you like tomorrow?"

She made a joyous sound and hugged me while I was driving, forcing me to concentrate on steering so I wouldn't go off the road. When she realized what she had done, she said, "Sorry, I guess I shouldn't have done that."

"Yeah, probably not!" I laughed

The next day, at Mazur's Motorcars, Hannah immediately gravitated to a plain gray Subaru Outback, an all-wheel drive SUV with black wheels and trim. It was not the car I thought would appeal to her, but she loved its rugged utilitarian look. I had just learned something new about her. The numbers on the windshield advertised the price at $9999, but when we went inside to make a deal, Bill Mazur wrote down a number that was just over half that, plus tax and plates, with a twelve-month warranty.

Hannah was thrilled with the car, and I was delighted with the price. He told us he would have his mechanic go through the car completely, and we could take delivery the following day. Before leaving, Hannah took a few pictures to show her friends.

CHAPTER 31

During the month of June, we followed the case against the racist White Plains cops daily by watching the evening news. It was always the lead story, and every few days, the media would obtain a quote from FBI Special Agent Meyers of the Westchester Field Office about the case's progress. On one occasion, he told us that John Maddox, the other cop involved in Jerome's beating, would testify for the prosecution in exchange for reduced charges.

Each week, another victim would come forward with their story of how one of these men had brutalized them over the last several years. There was plenty of material for the media to keep the story front and center.

Mia and I left for our sailing trip on the first of July. Over the next few weeks, we picked our way through Long Island Sound, stopping wherever looked appealing. Some of our favorite stops were where we could anchor in secluded bays, enjoy a nice dinner aboard, and go skinny dipping after dark. After Mia was comfortable in the boat's galley, she was able to prepare many of her signature meals.

Eventually, we made it to Block Island, where Hannah took a ferry to meet us. While there, we enjoyed the beaches, toured the island on bicycles, and enjoyed fresh-shucked oysters. We usually finished our days drinking mudslides at the Oar Restaurant, overlooking all the boats. After hanging out there for a few days, she sailed with us to Newport, Rhode Island, and went home from there. A few days later, Judy met us in Newport, where we dined in fine restaurants and shopped in all the harbor-front stores. Judy sailed with us to Martha's Vineyard, where we explored the island for most of the week before she flew back to New York.

Mia and I worked our way home over the remaining few weeks, stopping wherever looked interesting along the Connecticut shore. During the trip, we kept track of the case on the internet. It was a story the media would not let go of. Besides the kidnapping and hate crime charges, Owens and Bruno were charged with other crimes for their role in the January 6 insurrection at the Capitol in Washington, DC.

When we returned home, the United States Attorney had scheduled a trial for mid-September. One morning, just before Labor Day, I called Seth for the inside scoop.

He said, "None of these guys has the money for a long, dragged-out federal trial. There are plea negotiations taking place, and my guess is they'll plea out, looking for a sentence of between five to ten years."

"Five years in prison for racist ex-cops will be no picnic," I said. "You've got that right. In addition, their pensions have been revoked, so they'll be broke when they get out."

"I'm good with that; how about you?"

"For sure. My goal, all along, has been for the Jordan family to be compensated for their loss. My negotiations with the city continue, and it looks like we'll end up with something north of five million."

"That's great, Seth. Are my guys and I going to have any issues?"

"No way. The media has made you out to be heroes!"

"That's good to hear, Seth. We'll be watching the news."

"Bye, Dan. Keep in touch."

Two weeks later, the United States Attorney for the Southern District of New York held a press conference. Everything turned out exactly as Seth had predicted.

THE END

ACKNOWLEDGMENTS

A special thanks to my early beta readers, Jennell Brown, China Powell, and Kristian Wilson Colyard. Another great cover by Temitope. Kessiah Carlbon, my website designer. Lawrence Butler, editor and proofreader, whose work was essential. And Trisha Fuentes, who did the formatting for publication. A big shout out to my writing gurus, Gabi Coatsworth, Tessa Smith-McGovern, and Marcia Bradley. And most importantly, I thank my wife, Beth, whose love and support make everything possible.

MORE TITLES BY LARRY TERHAAR:

OCEANSIDE

ONCE A DETECTIVE...

Follow the author at www.larryterhaar.com
FB- larryterhaarauthor

www.ingramcontent.com/pod-product-compliance
Lightning Source LLC
Chambersburg PA
CBHW072105300726
48975CB00003B/706